CRYING IN THE CHAPEL

CRYING IN THE CHAPEL

A
Swinging
Sixties
Mystery

Teresa Trent

Chapter One

August 1965

Camden, Texas

New life is amazing. I placed a hand on my cousin Ellie's midsection as we sat in a meeting in the Camden Chapel. Bloop. There it was. Just a slight push against my hand, and then nothing.

"That's wonderful. Does it do that often?"

Ellie grinned, and her face looked different. This wasn't the girl I swam at the lake with, or the girl who snuck me into the movie theater when she worked as a ticket taker, or even the woman who stood next to me when we saw JFK shot from an upper window in the Texas School Book Depository that November day in Dallas. Her face had changed. Angular features had become softer with the baby weight, and she seemed calmer about everything. She appeared at peace. Until she opened her mouth.

"Ow! Slow down, baby. I tell you, this kid just kicked what had to be a forty-eight-yard field goal. It never stops. When he gets the hiccups, he keeps me up all night."

Vernice Schaeffer, a woman in her early forties who wore tight, floral print dresses that accentuated her middle, chuckled as she cleaned her cat-eye glasses. She served as a coordinator for all the different people involved in the wedding. Her role was strictly volunteer, but she happily oversaw every single wedding in the church. "Oh, my dear, you'd better get used to that kid waking you up at night. I had two of them, and I can tell you the first one could have been a night shift worker, given the hours he kept. Of course, there were a couple of nights when my sweet Eddie took over. He didn't have to. He worked all day, but still he helped out. Somehow, the good Lord knew what he was doing when he gave me a man like that."

Replacing her glasses, she picked up a paper fan left from the funeral of Goody Mills, a local baker found dead in her kitchen after baking her signature icebox cookies. Goody's face beamed at me on one side, and her eyes seemed magnified behind a set of thick lenses. On the other side, a picture of the face of Jesus and the name of the funeral home waved through the air at me. Goody, Jesus. Goody, Jesus.

As awful as the fan was, I wished I had one. The August Texas heat had closed in, blanketing us in humidity, and it felt hard to breathe in the stuffy Sunday school room of the Camden Community Chapel, though the windows were open.

Davita Ross, the wedding soloist and wife of the officiating pastor, gazed at herself in a tortoiseshell compact mirror. She snapped it shut. "Pastor and I will never have to worry about that. Though some people think it's expected of a pastor and his wife, we are not having kids. We have enough to do."

All eyes turned to her, causing her to squirm slightly as she quickly finished. "Besides, did you hear about someone trying to kidnap that pregnant woman over in Bexar County? That's enough for me to stay just the way I am. Running the church here. It's a lot more work than you would think."

"That's you, Davita." The organist, Charlotte Koch, clapped her hands in excitement. "I think Ellie's upcoming bundle of joy is exciting. So, Ellie, do you really feel like it's a boy? You're carrying a little high and you know what they say—that means a boy."

Ellie laughed with a little snort. "Miss Charlotte, I realize it's 1965 and we are practically in the Space Age, but the only way we'll know is when this little rocket ship lands."

"Which should be in the next few weeks," I added.

"Oh my." Clarence Shellhammer, the choir director, spoke up. "If you are having a baby, how do you plan to fulfill the role of matron of honor?"

Ellie, in her Texas drawl, said, "Haven't thought that far, but somehow, I'll find a way. I can't let down my little cousin Dot on her special day. Where there's a will, there's a way." I had no doubts that even labor wouldn't stop her. When it came to being stubborn and loyal, Ellie was the queen.

I only hoped she was right. In two weeks, I would marry the love of my life, Ben Dalton, on August the fourteenth. What could go wrong? The day after Friday the thirteenth. I had never been overly superstitious, but I figured it was best not to take any chances.

"I agree with you, Davita." Clarence flashed Davita a friendly smile. "Did you read in the paper about the young girl over in Fort Worth who was almost kidnapped? Lucky for her, she realized something wasn't right when she was walking down the street, and a man offered her a ride. This world doesn't seem safe for you young ladies," Clarence said.

Vernice was still fanning up a storm, but none of her hair moved, held firmly in place under the power of hairspray. "Isn't that the truth."

"It was real near where my combo was playing," Clarence said.

"You also play with a group in Fort Worth? I didn't know that, Mr. Shellhammer," Ellie said.

Clarence beamed. "I'm more than just a choir director. I've been doing gig work with a couple of friends of mine for years. Sometimes we perform at clubs, while other times we do private events like weddings, or one time we did a car show. Our piano player, Kermit, does all our front work. He's pretty good at it, too. The night someone tried to take that girl, Lionel was out for a smoke between sets and heard her screaming. The cops got there pretty quick."

Vernice scowled. "How did she figure out she was about to be kidnapped by some man offering a ride? It doesn't make sense. I think you and your fellow musicians were partaking in those between-set cigarettes, and I don't mean the kind Pall Mall makes."

Clarence paled, "I'm insulted by your implication, Vernice, but I can assure you my report is accurate. *The Dallas Morning News* confirmed the story."

"And how did they know?" Vernice asked.

Clarence scooted back his chair. "It's silly of me to try to communicate with you on an intellectual level, Vernice. I keep forgetting you are not capable of intelligent discourse."

Charlotte had a wicked look in her eyes. "I wouldn't worry about it, Vernice. We all know you're safe."

Here I was, sitting in church, a place that is supposed to be peaceful and loving. But not when Clarence and Vernice were in the same room. This chapel of love felt more a house dominated by competitive siblings. Pastor Ross quieted them both down, and Vernice got back to business. Once everyone had given their reports, the meeting ended.

Before Ellie and I made it to the door, Vernice grabbed my hand. "I do hope your fiancé can make the next meeting. It really is better when only one person in the relationship doesn't have to do all the work."

Vernice's hand was sweaty from sitting in the hot room. I fought off the compulsion to pull my hand away and rub her sweat off on my shorts. Her words sounded well-meant, but they were edged with a hint of judgment. "Sorry. He'll be here. We're just so busy with the new house and getting ready for the wedding."

Vernice nodded. "Very good, then."

After the meeting, Ellie had to leave to help her one employee, Barbara, at Bluebonnets, Ellie's dress store. She had always loved to sew, and her special occasion dresses brought women from all over the state. We were shocked when Lady Bird Johnson and her daughter Lucy came shopping one time. Lucy needed dresses for events in Washington, D.C., and Ladybird told Ellie that Bluebonnets had been recommended to her by friends in Texas. She was in Texas managing her businesses, but made a special trip to Camden to look at the dresses on Ellie's rack. This year, Ellie had done record sales during the summer bridal season, and as she got closer to her due date, she relied more heavily on her one employee and her mother, my Aunt Mavis.

Ellie had been reluctant to pull Aunt Mavis into the business because my aunt had a way of running everything like a military maneuver. She had served with the WACs in WWII, and her military experience of structure, rules, and tight corners spilled over into everything she did. She had served as a nurse in Normandy and also worked in Birmingham in the United Kingdom. Her organizational style and nursing efficiency had probably saved a lot of lives, but carrying that much enthusiasm over into civilian life didn't always work, especially when it came to her daughter. Ellie had her own business because she enjoyed being her own boss. Letting her mother in had so far been the most troublesome part of baby preparations.

I entered the empty chapel holding a white leather bridal planning notebook, gifted to me by my own mother. The sturdy three-ring notebook held sections for guest lists, food, and the venue, and in the back pocket, my mother had included a small book from Emily Post, the etiquette goddess, on how to handle anything from duplicate gifts to late guests. Parts of the book were straight out of the Fifties, and things modern people in the Sixties rarely adhered to, but somehow it was good to have a book to tell me where the forks went in a place setting or how to properly plan a big event. Turns out, wedding planning involves a million different decisions, and today, I was working on the flowers. I decided my primary flower would be white daisies with other flowers worked in around them. I wanted the bouquets, the church, and the reception to be bursting with Gerber daisies. The best part was, they would also be on my wedding gown.

The Camden Chapel sanctuary was relatively small and could hold up to one hundred and fifty people. There were classrooms and offices situated on the other side of the church, and surprisingly, there were three floors. It had been a big building project for a town as small as Camden, but hope springs eternal that the heathens from the Dallas area will choose to commute and live in our bedroom community. My assignment from Vernice was to pick up frames that would hook onto the pews to allow the florist to arrange flowers on the end of each row. After retrieving the frames, I was to deliver them to Lily Salem, the florist. Ben suggested her because he knew her from the private school they both attended. She had recently moved to town and opened Lily's of the Field at the end of Main Street. For decades, Camden's only flower shop was Henley Flowers, and they were still going strong. When I worked at the funeral home, I had daily chats with Gertrude Henley, and they were excellent at delivering on time. It would be tough for a new flower shop to get established in Camden, but we hoped our wedding would give Lily's new business some good exposure.

Up front, standing on a metal stepladder, was Earl Gunther, the church caretaker. Vernice told me to ask him about these contraptions she called pew hooks. Earl was in his late fifties, with a slightly receding hairline that lent itself more to white than grey. He wore brown overalls with black buckles over a tan button-down shirt. He was replacing a lightbulb in the fixture that hung from the vaulted ceiling. His hand rested on the top of the ladder as he turned the bulb in the socket.

"Excuse me," I said in a quiet voice, not wanting to make him jump and possibly fall off the ladder. At his age, a fall could do some damage. "Are you Earl?"

"Yes, ma'am. How can I help you?" His voice was gentle and measured, like a kindly grandfather.

"Vernice told me you could get some pew hooks out of the closet somewhere?"

He descended the ladder. "Are you the new florist or the bride-to-be?"

I blushed. In the last month, I had picked up a new name. People now referred to me as the bride before they used my name. They grinned at me when they said it and I wondered what they were thinking. "I'm the bride. I'm Dot Morgan."

"Nice to meet you." He put a finger to his temple and repeated my name. "Dot Morgan. Why does that name ring a bell?"

"I'm not sure. I'm not a member here. My fiancé is Ben Dalton."

He shook his head. "No. That's not it." He stepped back slightly and focused on my face. Suddenly, he snapped his fingers. "That's it. I saw your picture in the paper. I have a knack for remembering things. That's what made me a good patrolman so many years ago. People would say stuff, mostly drunk people who were trying to drive, and then forget what they said. I didn't forget."

"You were a policeman?"

"Oh yes. Twenty-five years. I joined the force after a stint in the army. I mostly did patrol. I've brought half this town to the drunk tank, and I know about every husband and wife who fight so much that the neighbors call, too. I retired back in '57. So, how do I know about you?"

As he observed me like a man looking for a piece to a jigsaw puzzle, I shifted from one foot to the other. I was never comfortable when someone connected me to those articles. I had been in the paper several times, mostly having to do with catching killers. The thought of it sounded like something out of *The Fugitive* on TV. Once people put it together that I was *that* girl, they treated me differently, and sometimes worse, even acting differently around me. They were waiting for me to find out something they might be hiding. My parents' mailman once asked me if I knew what was happening with Mrs. Hitchcock down the street. I told him I didn't really know her, and he laughed and said, "But I hear that when you don't know, you have a way of finding out."

Was there something nefarious going on with Mrs. Hitchcock? I had no idea, nor did I want to find out. But the mailman imagined me as a clandestine source of information, brimming with details about the lives of Camden's people.

"Hey, Earl," Clarence Shellhammer said from the door. "I need to talk to you about something." He motioned for Earl to come closer.

"Excuse me," Earl said. He stepped to the back of the sanctuary, and the two men began to whisper. Clarence looked very bothered and kept pointing to the front of the church. I heard the word "pipes" and then, very clearly, that Earl needed to mind his own business.

Earl nodded and whispered something I couldn't hear. Then he smiled and patted Clarence on the arm. Clarence pulled away. And then looked over to me. "Sorry for interrupting."

As Clarence left, Earl turned and pointed a finger at me as he walked back to where we had been talking. "You were involved with that murder out at the lake. From what I read in the paper, you practically solved that case for the police." He smiled, making friendly creases on his cheeks. "You're a smart girl. Good to see a young woman who is as smart as she is pretty."

I wasn't sure what to say to that, so I mumbled out a thank you. He stared at me for a few more seconds and then suddenly nodded, remembering my request. "Right. I'll get those pew hooks for you, Detective Dot."

"Although a friend of mine is on the police, I'm not a detective, Earl. I'm just a secretary. An out-of-work secretary, right now."

Earl's head bobbed back slightly as a look of surprise came over his features. "You're too humble. I'm a good judge of character. And as far as just being a secretary, young lady, you just never know what you are capable of until you stop judging yourself."

As he walked away, I fought rolling my eyes at the moniker Detective Dot. How silly. Plus, I hated to admit how much I enjoyed hearing it.

Chapter Two

That evening, I met Ben at Columbo's, our town's well-loved Italian restaurant. We had spent many delightful evenings over a bowl of Columbo's spaghetti bolognese. Tonight, though, was different with the stress we were feeling. Even with Frank Sinatra's solid gold hits streaming over the speakers, our date was more like a meeting of parade officials the week before the balloons went up in the Macy's Thanksgiving Day Parade. Sinatra began singing about a kick in the head, and it was the perfect theme song for our mood. I thought I was feeling overwhelmed, but Ben was much worse, sounding like a doctor performing major surgery.

Ben speared a piece of lettuce from his Caesar salad. "So, you met with Vernice, and she has everything under control?"

I nodded while breaking apart a piece of garlic bread. "Check."

"And the music?"

"I'm working on it. I'm having trouble deciding." When I was younger, I thought about the song "True Love," especially because I loved the way Bing Crosby sang it to Grace Kelly in *High Society*, but now there was other music that warmed my heart. Hopefully, the song choice would come to me.

"That's not like you, but I know it's important to you to find just the right song."

"It is. And your best man, Dusty, is coming in on Friday so he can go to the bachelor party, right?

Ben nodded. "Oh, yeah. I can't wait for you to meet him. Remember, I told you we roomed together in college for three years, so he feels more like the obnoxious brother I never had. He's going to love you. He's coming up from

Houston. You know he helped with the opening of the Astrodome, right?"

"I didn't know that. What did he do?"

"He's part of the publicity department. He's the one who suggested they make the grounds crew wear futuristic space suits on opening day. All about the Astrodome theme. Did you know they put translucent paint on the dome so the grass inside could grow? That place is a wonder."

"Yeah, I heard it called the Eighth Wonder of the World. Is that true or did Dusty make that up?"

"I think it's true, but you might want to double-check that with the reference librarian at the library."

"I'm looking forward to meeting him, if for nothing else, hear some good stories you'd never dream of telling me. Is he really six foot four?"

"Yep. Tallest guy on campus. You would think a guy that big would be a brute, but he was a teddy bear. That's why we lived together for as long as we did. I knew he was easy to get along with most days. As for the stories, I was pretty boring in college."

"I'll be the judge of that." I wiggled my brows. If Dusty was as nice as Ben said he was, he'd have a good and maybe embarrassing story about their college days.

Joe Columbo came over with a bottle of red wine. "I hear someone is getting married in the next week. I have your invitation on my desk. Seeing as you two have spent so much time here, I feel partially responsible for your happiness. *Che la vostra casa sia sempre piena di risate, amore e calore.* May your home always be filled with laughter, love, and warmth." He opened the wine and poured a glass for Ben, who took a sip and nodded.

"Thank you so much, Mr. Columbo." I rose and hugged him, and then kissed him on the cheek.

"What's this Mr. Columbo business? Call me Joe."

"Joe. We love it here, as you can tell."

"You are like family, Dot and Ben. When the little ones come, we will pull out the highchairs and treat them like grandchildren."

Ben laughed. "Let us get married first."

"First comes love, then comes marriage, and then comes the little bitty baby carriage," Joe sang as he walked away, snapping his fingers.

His lovely gesture and the mention of our impending future plans brought Ben back to the task at hand. He took a breath and continued with the checklist right where we left off. "What about the flowers? Did you talk to Lily? You didn't forget, did you?"

"Yes, Ben. I talked to her. Settle down. Most grooms leave everything up to the bride. You're more worried about the details than I am."

Ben rubbed at the space between his eyes. He looked tired. "I know. Sorry. It's just that my mother has been ringing my phone off the hook."

"Why doesn't she call me instead? I can tell her firsthand what's happening."

"She doesn't want to do that. She doesn't want you to feel like she's interfering. She said a woman should plan her own wedding. After all, you only get one."

I struggled with this. My mother was engaged in the wedding planning. Why wasn't she? I hadn't spent much time with Ben's mother, Leslie, yet, and working on the wedding would give us a chance to get to know one another. I also felt that even if she was calling Ben to check on things and not me, she was still involved, just in a kind of sneaky way. What did that say about our future together? Would she always correct my mistakes through Ben?

"You're busy at work, Ben. Really, you can leave most of the wedding planning up to me. It's surprising how wound up you are about it. So, what if we miss something on your mother's list. She'll survive. After all, it's technically our wedding."

Ben winced and then said, "You're right. It's just that she reacts to things because of experiences she's had in the past."

"What experiences? She's a housewife who, from what I can tell, dotes on you and your father. Have you and your mom gone around about something else that I don't know about?" It was interesting how much you learn about a person when they are under stress. It seemed that Ben had occasional problems with his mother.

"It wasn't about me, but my aunt. My mom expected her to meet a guy, get married, have kids, and all that."

"And she didn't? What's wrong with that?"

"She wanted her sister to be like her. It's hard for her to accept that my aunt is very happy in her life. Sometimes I think she's happier than my mom. She has friends, she travels, and she's a contented person."

"What does she do?"

"Aunt Joanie is a teacher. She teaches high school English in San Antonio. She loves her kids and her school and tells my mom she doesn't feel the need to find a man."

It all made sense to me, now. Leslie's desire for the perfect wedding and her intense pressure on Ben to make it happen.

"What's your aunt like?"

"I love her. She's fun, and well, we both love to write, so we have that in common. She's part of the reason I went into journalism. She's in her fifties now, and still very active in local politics and goes to her school's football games."

Football in Texas was the thing most worshipped after God, with fewer potlucks.

"Her school went to state a few years ago. She went to all the out-of-town games as well as the home games. There's nothing special about my aunt except that she just chose a different life than her sister. My mom has trouble understanding that. She keeps saying that one day Aunt Joanie will show up with a handsome man on her arm and give up teaching."

"I think I'd like to meet her."

Ben rubbed the side of his neck. "She'll love you. Besides, she'll be at the wedding, so you'll see her there."

"Good. I'm thinking your Aunt Joanie and my Aunt Mavis might make quite a pair. They both sound a little stubborn." I twirled some spaghetti on my fork and took a bite. Columbo made the best spaghetti I'd ever tasted.

"You might be on to something there," Ben said. "Also, Lily called me twice today. She's looking for the pew hook things?"

"I picked them off this afternoon. Earl, your church's caretaker, found them for me."

He finished his salad and pushed his bowl to the side. "Good. I'm really hoping our little wedding will give her a leg up in competing with Henley's.

Even though she grew up here, and now has a flower shop, she's the new kid in town. I was so surprised when she came in to put an ad in the newspaper for Lily's of the Fields. It's great she's creating arrangements for the wedding, but I have to admit sometimes it's a little weird."

"In what way?" I asked. This didn't sound good, and I tried to hide my mounting fear that he still had feelings for this woman. It was unfounded. I'd never been jealous of another woman around Ben.

Ben spread his clean napkin on the table. I had come to realize he did this when he had to say something he'd rather not. He began to fold it, never looking up at me. "We were a couple in high school. We went to prom together."

That wasn't that bad. I had a couple of prom dates of my own in the past. I couldn't imagine still having feelings for either of them. One was so egotistical he told me he thought he looked better than I did, and the other was my lab partner. Great brain, no spark.

I was feeling good until Ben continued speaking. "Three years in a row."

My gut clenched. Three years? That's forever in high school. We were weeks from the wedding, and here my groom was telling me his long-lost love had come back into his life to arrange the flowers? What other arrangements did she have in mind?

"Did you date her after high school?" I asked. He fixed his gaze on the napkin and didn't answer. I continued, "I guess I should ask if I am the first girl you proposed to or the second?"

He cleared his throat and then, as he perfected a corner on the napkin, mumbled, "The second, actually."

"The second? You two were engaged?"

"Yes, and no." He finally looked at me. "I asked, and she said yes, but she wouldn't wear my ring, and then, after a few weeks, she left town. She wrote me a note saying she felt she was too young to tie herself down by getting married."

My heart plummeted in my chest, causing fear grounded in hopelessness. Could this be him ending our future? "I appreciate your honesty in all this, but I need to ask. Do you still have feelings for her?"

He abruptly lifted his head and looked straight into my eyes. "No. Oh God, not at all. Please don't think that. My heart belongs to you and only you. Please don't ever think I don't love you. It would kill me." He took my hand in his and squeezed to reassure me.

His words helped calm me, but finding out Lily was this big a part of his past caused my first brush with wedding cold feet to materialize. It's pretty hard to compete with a first love.

Chapter Three

Two days later, on Wednesday, I sat in my car in front of the flower shop with the windows rolled down, waiting for Vernice. As much as I was trying to avoid Lily after Ben's confession, Vernice insisted the three of us meet to make sure I got just the right flowers.

In one of our many meetings, Vernice once told me, "No matter what craziness might be going on in the background of a wedding, guests won't know or even need to know if the chapel décor is perfect. They look at the perfect flowers, the dresses, and the well-rehearsed wedding party and assume everything is going smoothly. I've even pulled this off with a drunk bride who wobbled her way up the aisle, but of course, I won't reveal who that little lush was." She shared other wedding disasters she had expertly averted. If there was a wall of fame for crazy weddings, hers would be full of people whose names she'd never disclose.

Vernice walked up to my car window, her lips pinched together. She raised a penciled eyebrow and blinked. "Why on earth would you wait in your car on a day like today? It has to be over a hundred out here. Look how flushed your cheeks are."

There was no possible way I could share that I was putting off facing my fiancé's former high school sweetheart who dumped him right before the wedding, so I tapped on my white leather wedding planner. "Needed to do some reorganizing before we get in there."

She glanced at the book I was sweating on, but didn't seem to be buying my story. "If you say so."

"This book has been a lifesaver," I said, in an effort to convince her I wasn't hiding out from my boyfriend's old love. "I have numbers and notes from every person involved in the wedding. I even have a paperback copy of Emily Post's etiquette book."

She looked impressed. "I need something like that. Could I borrow your book, just to see how it's set up?"

The thought of letting it go shoved my senses into a small panic. "Uh, sure. Just not right now."

She put a hand to her forehead. "Lord, we'll melt if we stand here much longer. Let's go in, shall we?"

"Of course. Let's go look at flowers," I said, trying to sound like I was looking forward to this. I couldn't be further from the truth. Especially now that my hair was limp from sweat. I grabbed the pew hooks and hung them over one arm.

We opened a glass door and were immediately hit with circulating air from several oversized fans. It wasn't cool, but noticeably less stuffy than in my car. The smell of roses, gardenias, and jasmine lilted through the air and hit my nose all at once. The shop had flower arrangements perched everywhere on glass and white pedestals, and there was a cooler with cut flowers arranged in bouquets and corsages next to the counter. There was also a large white and red funeral spray on a metal stand with the words "Rest in Peace" on it. Lily had not returned to Camden and opened her shop when I worked at the funeral home, but if she had, we would have encountered each other several times a week.

A female voice came from the back room. "I'll be there in one second." As I looked around, I realized Lily's business was like Ellie's at Bluebonnets. She was a single woman who had opened her own business and was single-handedly running it. No husband with money to cover costs when business was slow. It was impressive. Her re-emergence in Camden right before my wedding, though, was doing nothing to calm my nerves. I had always felt secure in Ben's love for me, but admittedly, I felt challenged for the first time.

Lily must have been on the phone because the cord from the wall phone was stretched behind a set of wooden swinging saloon-style doors. "Thank you for calling," she said, very businesslike, as she came through the doors and placed the handset back on the base. She was petite and brunette and reminded me of Suzanne Pleshette in the movie *The Birds*. She had short hair curled on top so that it had a little height, and even though she wore a green florist's apron, you could still see a hint of a well-formed bosom. Her voice was low for a woman. Not a two-packs-a-day voice, but a sultry, sexy tone that made me question just how well Ben had known her in school.

"Sorry about that," she apologized. "People order flowers and then expect them to appear on the spot."

"I know just what you mean," Vernice said. "I help out organizing weddings at my church, and some people don't understand how much time things take." Vernice extended her hand. "I'm Vernice Schaeffer. Welcome to Camden. Hopefully, we'll be working on other special occasions together."

Lily shook Vernice's hand and then switched her focus to me. "Thanks for coming by the store, Dot."

I handed her the pew hooks, which she quietly placed on the counter. "Thanks for bringing those. When Ben told me he was finally getting married, I have to admit I was just a little bit jealous." Even though she was gorgeous enough to rate a Hollywood movie role, she was warm. Almost caring.

"No problem," I said.

Lily blushed. "You know, we were once an item back in the day."

"He told me," I said. I'm pretty sure I sounded normal, and none of my gushing insecurity was leaking out anywhere. Why couldn't Ben's old girlfriend be unattractive, or better yet, married with a slew of kids? This woman could have any man in town, and I hoped she hadn't come back to get mine. She was smaller than I was in stature but bigger in the bust. My guess was she was of Italian heritage, but I couldn't be sure.

"He would," she said. "That man is as honest as the day is long. I always admired that about him. I guess he'll always be the one who got away. I don't exactly make the best decisions when it comes to men. Anyway, let me show you my floral designs, and you can choose which arrangements tickle your fancy."

She pulled a three-ring notebook out from behind the counter and opened a page of photos from other weddings. The book reminded me of the portfolio Ellie kept in her store, a large binder filled with pictures of bridal and bridesmaid dresses she had created.

"Amazing," I said. "Did you make all of these?"

"Every one of them. I had a florist shop in Dallas before I came here. There was a lot of competition in that market, but I made a good living."

"These are beautiful." Vernice reached for one of Lily's business cards in a stand on the counter. "I'll just keep this for future weddings. If Dot's wedding is a success, you can expect to hear from me. What possessed you to give up your business in the big city and move back to little old Camden? I'm sure your profit margins won't be the same."

Lily dropped her smile for a moment, but then pulled it back on. "What can I say? I'm a small-town girl at heart. I missed the people here."

Vernice put both hands over her ample bosom that was yet again squeezed into a floral dress. Today's outfit featured blue peonies dancing on a pink background. "That is so sweet. Are your parents still here?"

"My mother is," Lily answered.

Vernice zeroed in on Lily with a pensive look. "I don't think I know her. Where does she attend services?"

That would be like Vernice. To her, everyone in town attended church every Sunday, and even those were in some sort of pecking order in her mind, period. Status in the community just depended on which congregation you chose to worship with. Things were changing. Especially with younger people. I wasn't sure if it was the Vietnam War or the impact of the dreaded rock and roll music, but attitudes were loosening up when it came to regular church attendance.

"My mother doesn't attend church," Lily said.

Vernice's mouth dropped open in shock.

Lily quickly added, "She's been…ill."

Vernice's mouth turned into a pout. "Oh my, I'm sorry to hear that, my dear. How long has she been under the weather?"

Lily looked uncomfortable at Vernice's intrusive questioning. I suspected Vernice's passive judgment was bugging her, and I felt the need to change the subject. I tapped at a picture in the book of arrangements Lily had given me. "Is this one hard to make?"

A look of gratitude came over Lily's face. "Not at all. What colors were you thinking?"

Vernice cut in without being directly asked anything. "Oh, her colors are white and yellow. She's doing daisies. Can you do work with that kind of flower?"

"Of course," Lily answered. "I like that idea. It's a classic yet feels modern. I've been seeing more daisies in things lately. Maybe you're on trend, Dot."

"I hope so. I've always loved them."

"Then we shall rain down daisies for your wedding," Lily agreed.

I pulled out my wedding planner to start making notes, and the three of us got down to business. Lily was beautiful and showed complete professionalism to her ex-boyfriend's fiancée, and yet she made me nervous. I could never carry off the va-va-va-voom that filled the air around her, yet I felt sorry for her. I wasn't even sure why. She seemed like a really nice person. I even wondered if we could have been friends.

"You know what I think would be just divine?" Vernice asked as we exited Lily's of the Field and the midday heat enclosed around us like a suffocating blanket. "I think we should really make a statement and pull out the candlestands. We've used them a couple of times before for weddings and they tend to"—she clicked her tongue and held up a thumb—"take it up a notch. What do you think?"

She could go on like this all day, and had. I thought it would be divine to immediately get out of the heat. A day with Vernice was like two days with anyone else. Her energy level wore me out, and it seemed there was no end to the jobs she had for me. Didn't this woman realize I did not attend her church and had no idea what the candle stands looked like? I checked my Timex. I had planned on visiting my mother at the library for lunch. With everything going on, I didn't want to be late. My getting married was changing things between us. I was going from being her only daughter to someone's wife. It made me more like one of her friends in a way, but I would always be her daughter. I needed to wiggle out of Vernice's divine plan and spend some time with Mom.

"Uh, sounds great, but do we need to do this right now?"

Vernice tutted. "We don't, but you have to realize, young lady, the clock is ticking on this wedding." She then put a finger to her chin and cocked her head to the left, as if giving me time to think about it. Was this a tactic she used with her children? Was that how she saw me? "It won't take long," she said in a sing-songy voice.

I let out a frustrated sigh. "Okay. But I have other things to do today." If I let her, she would take up my entire day. She confessed her husband was out of town and her boys were at camp, so my wedding was her priority. I feared it was also the thing that filled up a boring day for her.

She nodded and waved a hand in the air. "Don't I know it. My dear Eddie has been working so hard in the last month. The poor man would work himself to death if it meant providing for me and the kids. He's just that kind of guy. But when he works, that doesn't mean I'm not taking on a mountain load of responsibility for the boys. I'm thanking my lucky stars they're at summer camp until next week. Someday, when you have kids of your own, you'll be amazed at all the things you have to do just to keep them fed, dressed, and passing classes at school."

I feared if I didn't interrupt her soon, she would keep on telling me her troubles as I felt my shoes melting around my feet. I made a move to my car.

"I'll meet you at the church," I said, not waiting for her to agree. Once in the car, I used all my strength to roll down my window and then reached across the passenger seat to roll down the other. At least I could get a cross breeze. Once I got rolling, I lifted my hair to cool the sweat on the back of my neck. I was holding it up with one hand, the other holding the wheel.

Vernice, having gotten my message, got into her car and revved the engine, causing a series of strange clunking sounds to emanate from the hood. As much as she bragged about what a great guy her husband was, he didn't seem to be keeping her car in good repair.

As I drove the few blocks to the church, the wind blew through my hair. I had always been a natural blond, and over the summer, I had let it grow out from a pageboy cut. Ben liked my hair long. If I weren't getting married this summer, I would have cut it short, like Twiggy. Now it was down to my shoulders, and I planned to wear it up for the wedding. Only I planned to wear it without the half can of hairspray my beautician wanted to put on. Tease and spray, a Texas tradition. I firmly believed Tease and Spray would be a much more appropriate name for the beauty shop than Gloria's Glamour House.

Once at the church, I parked in the side lot and grabbed my bag, leaving my notebook on the passenger seat. Surely I wouldn't need it just to look at candlesticks. I rolled up both windows in case we had a summer thunderstorm and made my way around to the front of the church. The windows were open, and the sound of organ music floated across the breeze. Miss Charlotte was practicing Bach's "Toccata and Fugue in D minor" and had just launched into the upward spirals. I remembered the piece from watching the old movie *Dr. Jekyll and Mr. Hyde*. The melody still creeps me out to this day. Vernice pulled up next to my car just as I turned the corner to get to the front door of the church. During the week, this was the only door unlocked.

I was fumbling with my keys in my purse, the metallic jingle giving me a clue to where they were, when I noticed someone sprawled on the lawn. The person appeared to be sleeping, but as I approached, I realized one of his legs was bent at the knee at an unnatural angle.

I drew closer, and a blood-curdling scream split through the summer heat from behind me. Vernice had caught up to me and now had her hands on her cheeks, her face deep red, letting out a long, high-pitched scream that split my ears. When Vernice took a breath, a car motor could be heard grinding behind us. I steadied myself on the lawn of the church. Pastor Ross came running out of the open door, minus the sports coat he usually wore over his white shirt and pastoral collar. The toccata stopped abruptly, leaving all of us standing in silence after Vernice's scream.

"Vernice? What's wrong?" he asked.

Vernice, for once, had no words. Going from screams to shock, she now clutched at her throat and pointed to the ground.

The pastor's eyes followed her finger, and upon seeing the man on the lawn, gasped. He ran to the prone body and knelt beside him. "Oh my God, it's Earl."

Looking more closely, I realized it was the man I had spoken to yesterday when he was changing a lightbulb in the sanctuary. The pastor put a finger to Earl's wrist, then slowly raised his head. "I think, I think he's badly injured. Earl?"

He waited for Earl to answer, and when he didn't, he repeated his name. Still nothing.

"Did you see his leg?" I asked, not able to get past its bizarre appearance. The bend was unnatural.

The pastor dropped Earl's wrist and then looked up into the sky. What was he looking at? Did he think he fell out of a plane?

Following his gaze, I realized he was looking up into the church belfry that rose against the sky. The wooden and brick square frame that faced the town had four arched windows with a large bell hung in the middle. When the Camden Chapel bell rang, it could be heard all the way to the H-E-B grocery store.

"He had been looking for a leak up there," Pastor Ross said. "I thought he fixed it. Water was seeping through to one of the rooms upstairs." The belfry was three stories up. Camden Chapel was the tallest building in Camden and could be seen from all over town. Had Earl been working with the bell and fallen? He would have had to have been standing on the roof for that to happen.

Vernice was still out of it and kept backing up, her hand on her chest. Charlotte, the organist, now stood in the doorway.

"Vernice?" When she didn't answer, the pastor turned to me. "Can you run into the church and call the police on my phone?"

"Yes. Is he—" I couldn't say the word even as badly as I wanted to know.

"Yes. I believe he is. Now hurry. Please."

I ran across the lawn to the open door. I didn't feel the heat anymore. I kept seeing the body of the caretaker, the leg bent backwards.

Chapter Four

Twenty minutes later, everyone who had been in the church was now outside on the lawn watching the police investigate Earl's fatal fall while Vernice went inside to find one of the leftover fans from Goody's funeral. Probably needing to make a little distance between herself and the dead man. She hadn't returned yet. I'm sure she was still rattled from seeing Earl's lifeless body lying on the freshly cut grass, undoubtedly cut by him.

"I can't believe this has happened," Charlotte said as she took a long draw from a Virginia Slims cigarette, her hands shaking. "I've known Earl since the day I took this job. He always seemed so careful, especially when he was up in the belfry. He's in his fifties or sixties, but I didn't think he was that old."

She took another drag with shaking hands. Her mahogany hair held its shape in the heat. It was teased at the top, and the ends had been curled up into a flip. Her hazel eyes were lined with a fine black eyeliner, which tipped up slightly at the end of each eye.

"I didn't realize he was working in the belfry," Pastor Ross said. "He was trying to patch a leak but was having trouble finding where it was. I thought he was up in the attic, and I was worried about him with the heat up there, but that wouldn't stop Earl. He was dogged when it came to repairs around the place, and he never charged us a penny. He was married to Pastor Treadwell's daughter. Her father was pastor here before me. I don't know how I'm going to call her and tell her what has happened. This is not going to be easy."

"I'm so sorry," I said, comforting a man whose job it was to comfort everyone else.

I was glad to see my friend and Camden police officer, Mary Oliva, working as a member of the investigative team. Her new boss, Detective Barrerra, was walking around the lawn asking questions and writing things down. It didn't surprise me when he made his way over to where I was standing. "Well, if it isn't Camden's very own Nancy Drew." Detective Fabio Barrerra towered over me. He was the first Mexican detective the city of Camden had ever employed, and last spring, I was so grateful when he came on board after I had been butting heads with the misogynistic, racist detective who had been making Mary's life miserable. The same detective who had been more than happy to put me in my place. His ouster was a win not only for me but also for my dear friend, whom the former detective had demoted. Mary was a trained law enforcement officer and a darn good cop. But her former boss never let her take on anything beyond filing. Now, she was a respected member of the investigative team. It seemed the all-male department had a history of thinking women were only good for getting coffee, filing, or other administrative and housekeeping tasks. Mary was smarter than anyone I knew, and at this moment, she was crouching over Earl's body, taking notes.

"This is a pretty big church for a little town like Camden. Did anyone see him fall?" Barrerra asked while looking up to the belfry. He switched his focus to our small group.

I shook my head while Charlotte dropped her cigarette and stubbed it out on the church lawn with the toe of her shoe. "Nope. I was playing the organ, so I didn't see or hear anything. I didn't even know he was up there."

"For what reason would he be in the belfry?"

Pastor Ross cleared his throat while his wife, Davita, who had walked over from the parsonage, quickly took hold of his hand. "I'm not sure, but he might have been repairing the floor in the belfry. We had a leak."

Barrerra's eyebrows rose as he made eye contact with everyone in the group to confirm the pastor's words. Charlotte shrugged her shoulders, and I did the same.

"Can you describe the belfry area to me?" He directed his question toward me. "I'm on my way up in a few minutes, but I'd like to get your take on what to look out for. Are there loose areas or railings where someone could fall through?"

I replied first. "I'm getting married here, but this isn't my church. I've never been up in the belfry."

He nodded. "Congratulations. Mary didn't tell me."

"Thank you."

Charlotte looked up to the belfry. "I love the sound of the bell on Sunday morning, but I've never actually been up there. I know there's a stairway behind the altar in the sanctuary."

"I've been up there many times." Pastor Ross shook his head. "It's perfectly safe. The only way to fall out of that belfry is to jump, and I don't think Earl would do that."

"With all due respect, pastor, sometimes people do things that surprise us. Had Earl been despondent about something? Had he had a big disappointment in his life that he shared with you? How about his marriage? Was that going okay?"

The pastor looked confused. "As far as I knew, everything was going fine in Earl's life. He had been happily married for over thirty years. You know he used to be a policeman, right?"

Barrerra's lips thinned. "Really? Here in Camden? Well, now, that is a shame. Also, being a cop and happily married don't always fit well together, especially after thirty years. If you have his address handy, I'll have one of my officers notify his wife."

Pastor Ross nodded. "Yes, I do. If you don't mind, I'd like to come along when you tell her. It might be a little easier coming from me. Also, his mother lives with them. She'll have to be told."

Barrerra gave a little bow. "Of course. That's very thoughtful of you."

Mary then came over, a slight smile on her face. "And here you are. The person most likely for me to run into at a crime scene. I'll bet they even put that in your high school yearbook." She gave me a quick hug.

"Right now, officer," Barrerra said, "this is not officially a crime scene. It's an accident scene. We'll look around a little bit more, run some tests, and confirm what I suspect was merely a fall."

Her attitude changed quickly, becoming more professional. "Yes, sir."

He turned to Charlotte. "Could you show me where the door is to the belfry?"

"Sure thing," she said. "Follow me."

Davita and Roger Ross trailed them and re-entered the church.

As the two of them walked into the church, Mary drew me close. "If I had to put money on it, the guy was pushed. He was murdered."

"It sounds like Detective Barrerra thinks he might have jumped. He was asking if he was depressed. You think he was murdered? Why would you say that?"

"Call it instinct. He looks old enough to have been in a war. If he had, he might know that when you jump out of a plane, you fold your legs slightly, tuck in, and roll. He landed like a rag doll."

"You're right. He told me he served in the army before joining the police force. Even so, it seems like a lot of theory, not too many facts," I whispered back.

"It's just a feeling. I didn't know he was a cop. I'll have to ask some of the old timers to see if they remember him."

"If you get to go up there, tell me what you see. Your boss is right. How does a man go from working inside to falling off the outside of a building? I just talked to Earl a few days ago when he helped me get the floral hooks for the pews. He seemed perfectly fine to me. As a matter of fact, he paid me a compliment. He told me I was a smart girl. He'd read all the articles in the paper I'd been included in."

"What can I say? You're a local celebrity around here. Trust me, Dot. Something isn't right here. This was not some kind of work accident."

Mary's gut feelings were often correct. That's why she was so good at her job. Once the Camden police saw past the color of her skin and the fact she was a woman, they realized it too.

A car screeched into the parking lot, causing both of us to turn. Ben jumped out and ran to where we were standing on the church lawn. "We got word someone died here?" He turned to me, and gently touched my elbow. "Are you okay?"

"Yes, it was the caretaker. He fell from the belfry."

Ben got a skeptical look on his face. "And I'm just guessing here, but could it be you found him?"

"It could," I answered, looking at my feet.

"She sure did," Mary interrupted. "And we already have suspicions."

Ben looked up to the belfry. "Was it an accident? Is that what the police think?"

I shrugged my shoulders, "At this point, it sounds like it."

Ben put his palm to his forehead. "Here we go again. And you think?"

"I think it's too early to tell." I smiled at Mary. I also wonder what had really happened to poor Earl Gunther, the church caretaker?

Chapter Five

After everything that happened at the Camden Chapel, Pastor Ross called me to make sure we weren't backing out of our venue reservation since the church was now not only a house of worship but also the scene of a questionable accident. He made sure I didn't forget that Vernice had been working very hard to pull our wedding off, and he would hate to see it all go by the wayside and have us getting married at the courthouse.

I assured him we were planning on exchanging our vows at Camden Chapel. "We talked about it, and, well, Ben's parents really want us to get married at the church. So, it's a go."

"Glad to hear it. I thought it might be best if we had a little meeting to check in with everyone and make sure everything is still going smoothly. We're all a little bit shaken up from Earl's death. Not only was he a dear friend, but he also took responsibility for the church's upkeep. I'm trying to find if he kept any logs of repairs and maintenance, and who he used when he couldn't fix a problem himself. It will be a long time before we find another church member who wants to volunteer that much time. I'm afraid we'll have to start hiring out. Anyway, let's all touch base so we can make sure your wedding goes off seamlessly," the pastor said.

Another meeting seemed like overkill, but I knew committee meetings were the lifeblood of church business. "Uh, sure, we can do that, but it hardly seems necessary, Pastor. Vernice has everything under control."

"Jesus went after that one little lost lamb, and I have to make sure that all my lambs are doing all right after…after what happened." Leave it to a pastor to never miss an opportunity to work in a Bible story. That night, Ben and I reported to the church for a 6:30 meeting. We were a little early, but could see that someone was inside the church. We sat in Ben's car with the windows rolled down, feeling a cooling breeze crossing over us.

I took Ben's hand and looked up at the belfry. "It seems so strange someone died from a fall right here in Camden. Is your church the tallest building in town?"

"It is." He peered up. "Do you think we have time to go up there before the meeting?"

I looked at my Timex. "We're twenty minutes early. I suppose we could."

Ben took the keys out of the ignition and pocketed them.

"What if someone stops us? We are going to be walking all over a crime scene." I said.

"I've grown up in this church. No one will stop me. I've been running around these halls since kindergarten. Besides, if you look like you have important business, nobody bothers you."

I let go of his hand, grabbed my purse, and got out of my side of the car. "If you say so."

When we entered the church, Ben tiptoed over to the sanctuary and looked in. The overhead lights were on, but there was no one inside. This was lucky, because every other time I'd been there, I'd run into someone. Ben put a finger to his lips.

"Don't make any noise," he whispered.

"I thought you said they wouldn't notice you?"

"Well, yes, but we're in church. Once you get into a place like this, doing anything wrong seems to be larger than it felt on the outside." He tiptoed into the sanctuary, and we made quick work getting down the aisle. Behind the organ on the left-hand side, Ben opened the plain white door that led to the belfry. As comfortable as the sanctuary felt, the darkened stairway to the belfry was hot, stuffy, and dusty. Ben ran his hand along the wall until he made contact with a light switch, which highlighted the dust motes in the air flying around us.

"This way," Ben said.

We climbed what seemed to be a never-ending flight of tightly curved steps until we reached a door at the very top. Ben jiggled the doorknob. The church might have decided to lock it after what had happened, and I worried we had endured all the dust for nothing. With a slight push, the door gave way. We were in.

The evening sun was setting on the horizon, and the homes and businesses of Camden were lined up in neat little rows as its inhabitants readied supper and did evening chores before bed. There was smoke coming up from the diner, and a baseball game was in full swing over at the park as the sound of a bat hitting a ball sliced through the air.

"It's beautiful up here," I said as I leaned over the wall of one of the archways. This time of day, our town looked like a scene straight from the play *Our Town* by Thornton Wilder. It was almost magical.

"You'd better be careful there, Dot. I don't know how sturdy that is," Ben warned me.

I looked around the structure of the belfry. If anything, considering how old the church was, it looked very solid. I went to the side Earl fell from, but this time, instead of leaning over the edge, I looked at the floorboards. We had been so surrounded by dust, but here the dust was very light. The sides were a mixture of rough-hewn boards and brickwork, and as I leaned closer to a brick in the enclosure, I found a small piece of metal. "What's this?"

"What's what?"

I held it up to Ben. "It looks like a curved piece of metal. The silver is bright, so it couldn't have been up here for too long." I held the metal sliver up to the zipper on my slacks. "Wait a minute. It's a zipper pull, but it's much bigger than the pull on my pants. See?"

Ben stroked his chin. "I think you're right. Do you think it came off Earl when he went over?"

"I don't know. I didn't think men's pants had pulls this big. I'll have to ask Mary if Earl had a broken zipper."

A metallic wheezing sound came from down on the ground with a final backfire that shot through the air. Vernice had just parked her nearly dead car. She opened the driver's side door, the squeak loud enough to make the dogs down the street go into a tirade of barking, sure they were being attacked by aliens.

"We need to get back downstairs," I said. "Vernice is here."

"We do," Ben said, then took hold of my hand. "But first," he pushed a strand of hair out of my eyes, put there by the evening breeze. "I never kissed a girl in a belfry before."

The magic of *Our Town* returned to my thoughts. What a lovely evening. I remembered a quote from the play.

Do human beings ever realize what life is while they're living it?—every, every minute?

Tonight, looking out on Camden and holding Ben in my arms, I realized that for right now, I did.

When we made it to the meeting, we found everyone involved in our wedding seated around the adult Sunday school table. We were treated to the full staff. The choir director, Davita, the pastor's wife, our soloist, the organist, and the choir director. If they'd had more chairs, I worried Pastor Ross might have pulled in the entire choir.

"Thank you all for coming today on such short notice," he started off, but Vernice quickly took over.

"We've had a tragedy in our congregation," she said, "but we also have a joyful celebration coming up. We need to do our very best to make sure that we are all still prepared to make Ben and Dot's special day happen. Can I get reports?"

Davita rolled her eyes at Vernice's take-command approach. Clarence shook his head in disgust, and Charlotte didn't seem to be listening, occupying herself with a knitting project, her light blue yarn ball rolling on the floor under the table.

Vernice didn't seem fazed by the lack of attention and quickly pivoted to me and Ben. "It never hurts to have a check-in right before a blessed event. First, let's go to the couple. Your matron of honor and best man are set? They have their outfits and have been briefed on their roles in the wedding and reception?"

"Yes," I answered. "Ellie is ready, and Ben's friend Dusty is coming in Friday.

He will be at the bachelor party and is preparing his best-man toast for the reception."

"And this Dusty"—she said the nickname as if it left a bad taste in her mouth—"or whatever you call him, is a reliable best man?"

Ben lifted his head. "He's the best. Why do you ask?"

Vernice's snobbery was caught out. "Oh, no reason. I will tell you that I've had some history with flaky best men who show up drunk to the wedding. Bridesmaids as well. I can't understand why people can't start drinking after the ceremony, not before."

"He'll be there and sober," Ben promised.

She turned to Clarence. "Is the choir ready with 'Beautiful Savior'?"

Clarence nodded, glanced quickly at Davita, then back to Vernice. "Of course, the choir is ready. We're professional volunteers and never take any gigs for granted. Weddings are a showcase for the choir and also an excellent recruitment tool for possible new members to the church." Clarence shared with me earlier that he was the bass player in a three-piece ensemble that played in Dallas, so he was comfortable using terms like "gig." Directing the choir helped pay the bills, because his true heart belonged to jazz.

"Very good," Vernice said. "And Charlotte? Will the organ music be ready?"

Charlotte nodded. "I've been playing these songs on the organ for years, Vernice. I don't even know why you called me in to this meeting." She resumed her knitting.

Vernice pinched her lips together. She was clearly not happy with Charlotte's lack of respect for her leadership. "Maybe so, but you are also accompanying Mrs. Ross, and I need to make sure that our soloist has well-rehearsed music to accompany her. One mistake will make the whole wedding look thrown-together."

Davita Ross sat quietly next to her husband but barely seemed aware of the surroundings. Her arms were crossed as she leaned back in her chair, her eyes looking out the Sunday school window. She was looking at the exact spot where the caretaker fell.

"And you, Davita?"

Davita did not answer until her husband reached over and gently touched her shoulder. "Darling," he whispered.

She jumped at his touch. "Oh, yes?"

Vernice leaned forward and spoke to Davita as if she were a small child. "I was asking if you are ready for the wedding."

Davita clearly didn't appreciate the way she was being spoken to and looked down her nose at Vernice. "I don't have a song yet from the bride, but as soon as I do, I will be ready to sing. Why do you ask?"

Charlotte let out a giggle, now happy she wasn't the target of Vernice's questions. "Because your attention seems to be elsewhere."

Davita scowled. "I don't know what you're talking about. I'm here, aren't I?"

A strange smile came over Charlotte's face. "And we are all very blessed by your beautiful voice."

Clarence came to Davita's rescue. "Davita's time is being wasted here. She could sing professionally anywhere she wanted, so this wedding will not be a problem."

Davita's cheeks reddened. "Thank you, Clarence."

Charlotte rolled her eyes after hearing Clarence's mush. "I wouldn't be surprised if she had her bag packed, getting ready to make her break for the big time."

Davita pushed her chair back. "I've answered your question. I have other things to do."

Ben whispered in my ear. "What are they talking about?"

I whispered back, "I have no idea."

Ben tapped on his watch. "We need to wrap this up. We're meeting my parents in half an hour."

I had almost forgotten about our dinner invitation. This little get-together with Ben's mom and dad made me even more nervous than thinking about my upcoming wedding. Ben's mother and I had been together on many occasions, but there was something that hadn't clicked between us. I could never figure out why.

"I can report that the outside vendors, the flowers, and the cake are all underway, and the bride's family will be taking care of decorating for the reception," Vernice said. "Our little group might have been shaken by the loss of our dear Earl, but we are all professionals, and we will make it through this. May Earl's soul rest in peace."

"Amen," the pastor said, and the assembled group echoed him.

As we left the meeting, I couldn't help thinking how strange it all was. These people got together just to make sure our wedding would be on course after Earl's accident, but it seemed a little unnecessary. I could understand their worries about whether we would want to have the wedding there, but a phone call would have sufficed. I had to suppose that in a church environment, meetings were a regular part of doing business, but none of the attendees seemed interested in giving reports on jobs they were doing already. At least it filled the time before dinner with my future in-laws.

Chapter Six

The first thing I noticed about Ben's childhood home was the smell of lemon furniture polish. Every surface gleamed. There was no clutter anywhere, and every tabletop contained either a lamp or a vase of flowers. A single-story structure, the house boasted cabbage rose wallpaper in several rooms, and others displayed plain stripes, accented with wood paneling, wainscoting, and slender rails. The temperature in the house was noticeably cooler, probably because of the three red oak trees in the front yard, which fully shaded every corner of the roof. There was also the comfortable hum of an air conditioning window unit, which had been installed in the den. I had to fight the urge to stand in front of it and let the air meant for an entire room be just for me.

Ben's mom ran in from the kitchen holding a bowl. "You made it." She wore a brown linen dress and an apron with matching brown pineapples printed on it. Even though she had been slaving away in a hot kitchen, she looked like a showroom model for the new line of Frigidaire. She was holding a bowl of mashed potatoes that resembled a ski slope from the soft, delicious ridges left by her mixer. The smell of pot roast followed her from the kitchen.

"Benjamin, be a gentleman and put these potatoes on the table for me, won't you?" Ben took the bowl, and as he did, kissed his mother on the cheek. She then turned her gaze to me. "We women will finish up in the kitchen. Your father is in the den with his newspaper. You know how he loves to read your articles." To accent just how special Ben's articles were, she wiggled her nose like Elizabeth Montgomery in the new television program *Bewitched*.

"Come with me, Dot, dear. A woman's work is never done. Clark and Ben can keep themselves occupied."

She crooked her finger over her shoulder as she led me to the kitchen. Was this what life was going to be like? The men relaxed in the den while the women worked their butts off in the kitchen? Ellie had subscribed to *Woman's Day* and *Ladies' Home Journal* once she and Al were married. She was suddenly concerned with being the perfect wife and homemaker, even though she was holding down a full-time job. She lived for the new recipes every month and announced to anyone who would listen what dish she would be making the next week. Would I be like that too? Hung up on the latest meatloaf recipe, or gauging my ups and downs on whether or not I could get rid of that nasty ring around the collar on one of Ben's shirts?

"I'm so glad you're here, dear." Ben's mom, Leslie, put her hand to her brow, rubbing away a shine of sweat. I'm just putting things in serving dishes. Can you put those green beans in a bowl?" She pointed to a series of empty bowls on the counter. "Then we need to put the bread in the basket, pour gravy into the gravy boat, and put out the salt and pepper, and slice the butter into pats. I'll let you handle that while I take the roast out of the oven."

Her list was overwhelming, but I tried to act like it wasn't. "Uh, sure. Glad to help."

Upon my acceptance, she wrinkled her nose again, and I decided it was definitely cuter when Elizabeth Montgomery did it. "Glad to have a helper."

I went through the list of tasks and delivered everything to the dining room table. Ben's and his father's voices drifted from the den.

"So, they think poor Earl fell out of the belfry? I've known that man for years. We've played golf on occasion, but mostly we've spent hours together at church potlucks. Was it an accident?" Clark asked.

"That's what they're saying," Ben answered.

Clark took a puff of his pipe, set it down in an ashtray, and then picked up a folded newspaper. Watching him, I decided Clark reminded me of Fred MacMurray from *My Three Sons*. Like the actor, he smoked a pipe and had a penchant for plaid. He was the all-American dad. Was I seeing a future Ben? Plaid and pipe, newspaper at the ready?

"If nothing else, Earl was a detail-oriented man. When we put in a new furnace, Earl called up all the furnace manufacturers: Lennox, Carrier, Rheem, and American Standard. And those were long-distance, mind you. But to him, the cost of the calls was worth it to make sure we got the most efficient unit. It's hard for me to believe he would make a careless error and fall out of a belfry. What do you think?"

"I'm not sure. I had no idea Earl was so meticulous about taking care of the church. That changes things. Plus, it seems like a strange way to die," Ben added.

"That's my boy." Clark picked up his pipe and gestured in pride with it. "You've already solved so many murders in this town. It's a wonder they don't have you working for the police."

Listening to this version of events bothered me. Ben's dad was giving him all the credit for past cases that we worked together on, and in some instances, I did alone. Was this how they saw things? Ben was the hero, and I was the little woman who put gravy in the gravy boat? I set down the bowl I was carrying and stepped into the den. I probably should have remained quiet, but I couldn't let his view of our detective work go uncorrected.

"You know, I had something to do with all of those cases, too." Ben's dad seemed surprised by my presence. He sat up straighter and turned his head abruptly, grinning. "Of course you were, sweetheart. It's just that Ben was there to rescue you. You can't forget that."

That was only partially true, and as much as I wanted to fire back, when I saw the look in Ben's eyes, I decided not to make an issue of it.

"Dinner's ready!" Ben's mother said from the doorway, and she removed her apron. "Let's eat."

We all followed her obediently to the dining room. Ben and I sat next to each other with Leslie and Clark across from us. Ben's father began carving the roast, and the slices fell gracefully to the plate like divers in a water ballet, perfectly tender.

"This is a work of art, Leslie," Clark said, complimenting his wife's cooking. Even though she had been cooking roast beef for decades, it was sweet that he still took a moment to appreciate her efforts. I was touched by his kindness to his wife. The table setting, loaded with entrées and side dishes, looked like it came straight out of one of Ellie's magazines. "You sure know your way around a kitchen," he continued.

She smiled and nodded as she carefully placed a white cloth napkin on her lap. "Thank you, but I had help tonight."

"I can't take credit," I said. "All I did was put your food into bowls."

Clark began putting pieces of meat on plates handed to him. "As it should be." He then flashed a smile at me. "I look forward to what you create for us in the kitchen when you have a home of your own. Like I've always said, a woman's heart will always be in the home."

I tried to keep the smile plastered on my face, but there was a little crack in my forced politeness. Always? Always in the home? I tried to count to ten but kept stopping at two or three. Ben's gaze met mine, and if eyeballs could talk, his were saying, "Let it go."

Nope.

"And a woman's heart might also be outside the home." It came out before I could stop it. I should have stayed quiet. The last thing I wanted to do was start a fight right before the wedding, but the things they were saying, and their assumptions about who I was and how I would act once I married their son, had weakened my resolve.

Leslie put a spoonful of potatoes on her plate. "In what way, dear?" She looked completely perplexed by the notion. It was clearly at odds with her idea of life for a new bride.

"Well," I started, but Ben's eyes widened, and I felt his hand gently squeezing my knee. I continued speaking. "I was working as a secretary before we got engaged. I enjoyed the work, and I think I was actually pretty good at it. I can type, file, manage an office, work on the phones, and help keep track of the books. I went to secretarial school to learn most of these things, but I've also learned on the job. It seems like an awful waste to give it all up, so I plan to keep working."

Ben's mother let out a little laugh. "Oh, darling, you can't be serious. You are taking on a full-time job as it is." Her tone was similar to one you would use with a small child.

"What would that be?" I asked.

"Taking care of our sweet Benjamin, of course. There's shopping, meals, laundry, and keeping the house clean. Doing those things right takes time. And then there will be the children. No, you have more than enough to do in your own little house." She then gave a curt nod as if saying, *End of discussion.*

"I'm not sure if you are aware of this, but I was raised by a working mother. My mom is a librarian at the public library. She took care of our home, like you say, but I was also expected to do chores around the house."

"Oh my," Leslie said. "That must have been difficult for you. What about your schoolwork?"

"I did fine. I made mistakes, but I also learned how to budget my time." I looked at Ben, who was buttering a roll and keeping his eyes downward. He was playing Switzerland on this and not taking anybody's side. "What do you think, Ben?"

"Uh, I think that, well, everything will work out in the end. I'm just happy to be getting married to the woman I love." His voice was soft and nonconfrontational.

Of course, he would say that. According to his parents, he was gaining his own personal staff to take care of his every need. What about me? Who was going to cook my dinner and iron my shirts?

Ben's mother reached over and lightly touched my arm. "I know it seems like a lot right now, but eventually, you'll come to see the home as your priority. It's the woman's gift to the partnership of holy matrimony. It's an adjustment for every young woman."

I looked down at my Betty Crocker-worthy potatoes and sighed. I had just ceased having a career. According to Leslie, my time was a gift to my husband. Ben squeezed my knee again. It was definitely an "I'm sorry" squeeze, but I wanted that sorry above the table in front of his mother.

Chapter Seven

The next morning, I woke to the sun shining through my upstairs bedroom window, and the day's heat had already begun to creep in. It was going to be another hot one, typical for August in Texas. I looked out at the sky, and a line of clouds was creeping into the idyllic blue. That's all it took. Just one dark cloud to mess up a perfect blue sky. It reminded me of the thoughts that seemed to hang over me and had me constantly worrying about the wedding. I had to start working on this anxiety. Everything would be fine, and the wedding didn't need to be perfect. I needed to redirect myself whenever I started fretting about things that had not happened yet. I focused on the birds singing outside. They were always excited for each new day. I could learn something from them. Even though I had things to do, I lingered for just a moment.

But here came one of those thoughts, barging in on a quiet, unguarded moment. I recalled my night before. Was it possible to have a hangover when you didn't drink anything? The words of Ben's parents danced around my head like stars in a Bugs Bunny cartoon. I had been walloped by June Cleaver with an anvil. How had I known Ben for as long as I had, but didn't realize that he came from a home that was a throwback to the fifties? The husband goes to work, and the wifey stays home and cleans, bakes, keeps herself attractive, and counts down the hours until his imminent return. I pulled the sheet up over my head. They couldn't really be expecting me to live that way, could they? It was 1965. Women could now vote, take birth control, and file for divorce, just like any man.

Pulling the covers down, I glanced around the room. The sun was streaming through the curtains, and the smell of freshly cut grass drifted in on the breeze. I could hear my landlady, Arlene, downstairs in the kitchen. She had been making jelly the last few days, and I waited for the smell of cooking fruit to come up the stairs. I would be sad to leave this apartment. Ellie and I had moved here together two years ago, both of us escaping living with our parents. It wasn't that our parents were all that bad, but being out on our own was a passage into adulthood for us. Technically, we were only a mile or two from our parents' houses, but it felt like we were in another city. Two women on their own. It had been a great move for Ellie because she and Al were getting serious, and swinging on her front porch with Aunt Mavis watching *Dragnet* in the living room wasn't exactly conducive to romance. Being several years younger than Ellie, I was just happy to be living on my own, holding down my first job, and feeling like an adult.

I'd grown up with Ellie, but living with her showed me what an independent woman looked like. More than just an independent woman, she was a *businesswoman*. She ran her own shop, dealt with customers, and almost always brought hand sewing home on the weekends. During this time, I went through several secretarial jobs, but she had figured out how to make it on her own without having to depend on anyone else. I admired her for that.

Now that Ellie was gone and I wasn't currently working, I was using my savings to pay rent until I moved in with Ben, when after that, he would pay the rent. I should have felt relief with the financial burden lifted, but I wanted more.

I was just as smart as Ellie, so why couldn't I create a stable income on my own? What did I need to do to prove to Ben's parents that just because I chose a different path outside of the home, I would be just as good of a wife for him? I feared they didn't listen to anything I said when it came to a woman's role in a marriage.

I shut my eyes for a moment. Maybe I could sleep through the day and handle the world tomorrow. It would surely be a nicer, kinder, more tolerant place by tomorrow.

Doubtful.

I threw back the sheets and jumped out of bed just as I heard the neighbor's lawn mower ratchet up. I needed to work on packing some boxes, and Ben was coming over to help me move a few things to our rental house. It was tiny with two bedrooms and one bathroom, but both sets of parents had glowingly called it our starter house. It was only one block down from Ben's parents, and I was beginning to think I might regret that decision. Would Leslie show up at random with a list of to-dos for me, or take it on herself to be my housewife coach, a la June Cleaver? This would not be pretty when I would have to tell her to back off, and I already knew I would.

I needed to talk to my mother about this. She had been where I am. My Grandma Morgan was a housewife her entire life. Had my mother had to convince her that being a librarian and raising a child was acceptable? She might be able to help.

When Ben knocked on the door a little bit later, I had several boxes packed, sealed, and sitting by the door for him to take downstairs. Arlene, who was in her kitchen, had skipped the jam today but was making up some lemon cake for her church's annual picnic. When we walked by, her face flushed, and her bottom lip quivered.

"I'm not going to cry," she said and then repeated, "I'm not going to cry."

I was pretty sure she was crying anyway. She had been excited when I told her I was engaged, right up until she figured out she would be losing me as a tenant. Her sadness was about more than the loss of income for her.

"I just don't know if I'll ever rent the apartment again. You felt more like family than a renter." This caused more tears, and that day I joined her. Arlene and I had become friends over the years. She was more than tolerant of Ben's visits, not something that ladies her age usually allowed. She felt like family to me, too.

When Ben and I got into his car, he asked, "Why is your landlady saying she's not crying? Is something going on with her?"

I leaned my elbow out the window to catch the breeze. "No. She's crying because I'm leaving."

He put the car in reverse and checked his mirrors. "Really? I didn't know you two were that close."

"We lived in the same house for two years. I helped her escape when her front porch caught fire. I don't know. So many things. I'll miss her." Sadness I didn't see coming suddenly hit me. It didn't take much for my emotions to take over these days. Was it the pressure of the wedding?

Ben squeezed my shoulder. "I know you will, but you'll be very busy in your new life as Mrs. Benjamin Dalton." I smiled but couldn't help feeling like I was hearing echoes of the night before.

"Mrs. Benjamin Dalton. That sounds official. Dot Dalton. That sounds like someone who reads the news on television." I put an invisible microphone up to my chin. "And here's Dot Dalton with the evening news."

Ben laughed. "That is funny. Dot Dalton. I'm just glad you won't get a job reading the news on TV. You'd put us all out of business at the paper. We all have perfect faces for radio."

"Thank you, I think. But why couldn't I get a job as a reporter on TV?"

Ben's eyes left the road for a minute and focused on me. He looked genuinely confused. "Well, I guess you could. You know, I think you can do anything. It's just that everyone who reports the news on television is a man."

He was right. Walter Cronkite, Edward R. Murrow, and that new guy who just started, Peter Jennings. All men.

"Then that's something that needs to change," I said, turning to face the breeze of the open window.

Why did it feel like I was stuck in the one step forward, two steps back trap? I'm employed, then I'm not. I'm engaged but now have to fight for independence.

We passed the Camden Chapel, and my gaze went to the spot where we had found poor Earl, the caretaker. There were no dents in the grass where his body had lain in the sun, yet I still knew exactly where he had landed. Mary was standing out on the lawn in the spot, looking up at the belfry.

I had work to do at the new house, but I couldn't resist what I really wanted to do, which was finding out what Mary was thinking about the crime scene. "Uh, would you mind stopping to talk to Mary? Just for a minute? The house is only a block away."

"Dot, I only have this morning to move boxes. I have to be at the paper at noon. We also need to ask Al about checking out those lights that aren't working right. Before I can do that, I need to check the lights in every room."

"I know, but just a minute." He blinked slowly as if in thought. We would be at the house in no time. The police had to be stumped figuring out whether the caretaker's fall was an accident or foul play, or Mary wouldn't be standing out there.

Ben didn't look like he wanted to stop, so I made a suggestion. "Why don't you drop me here, and I'll talk to Mary and then walk on to the house myself. That way, you can get a head start on your boxes."

He nodded. "Okay, but don't be too long. I'll start with the heavy boxes you couldn't lift anyway, but I need to get back to the paper before the deadline."

I saluted. "You got it. I won't be long."

He pulled into the church parking lot, and I jumped out of the car.

"Where's the rest of the police force?" I asked Mary as I made my way across the lawn.

Her long black hair was pulled into a bun at the base of her neck, and she wore the uniform of the Camden police. "What are you doing here?"

"Ben and I are moving boxes into the rental house, and I saw you looking at the church. Any new theories?"

"Yeah, I'm just trying to think about something," she said, her focus back up on the belfry. "We have some missing pieces on this one."

"What do you mean? It was an accidental fall."

"Not quite." She turned back to me and then looked over her shoulder to see if anyone was listening. "They found enough tranquilizers in his stomach to bring down an elephant. Someone drugged him and, from what I can tell, pushed him off. I thought it was strange the way his foot turned. You'd think someone who fell would land better. He fell like a rag doll, and now we know it was because he was unconscious."

I thought of my brief exchange with him. He was a nice, grandfatherly type who seemed like a man who would carry a spider outside rather than smash it. Who would drug him, then throw him off the third floor of a church? If he was murdered, it seemed like a pretty vicious thing for this crowd.

"I was trying to figure out exactly where he went off. It had to have been that opening." She pointed up. "It surprises me a little, because if I were going to throw someone out of the belfry, I wouldn't do it on the side that faces the street. They also did it in the middle of the day. I would have done it in the middle of the night and on the other side."

"It does seem strange. Maybe it had to do with opportunity. This was a better time for the killer."

"Maybe." She then faced me and put her hands on her hips. "But don't you have more important things to worry about, like a big wedding looming on the calendar?"

"Tell me about it. I think I made Ben drop me off here instead of helping him unpack boxes because I needed a break from all of it. You have no idea how looming is the exact right word."

"Come on, it can't be that bad. This is supposed to be one of the happiest days of your life. I know there are days when the sink is full of dishes, and the kids are fighting, that I wish I could go back to that day when my biggest concern was whether my Uncle Julio would eat all the appetizers."

"I wish I would have known you back then."

"Me too," she said.

"Let me ask you something, Mary. When you married John, were your in-laws expecting you to stay home with the kids?"

Mary laughed. "They knew better than that. If we were going to eat on a regular basis, it would take both of us working. It was a survival thing, you know, especially when we found out we were pregnant one month after the wedding. Why? Are Ben's parents telling you that?"

"Yes. I had no idea they were so traditional. I feel like I've landed in an episode of *Ozzie and Harriet*. My parents are great, and I guess I assumed everyone's parents were basically the same."

"But his aren't? That's hard to believe. Ben is a great guy."

"It shocked me, too. How could such closed-minded people raise a man like Ben? He's a journalist, and last I checked, people in that profession consider all sides of a story."

"So, tell them you are your own woman. This is your life, not theirs. You are starting a lifetime with them. You need to start on equal footing and with a mutual understanding of each other."

"I'm trying, but Ben keeps clamming up. I think he might actually want me at home ironing his shirts."

Mary blew out. "Not likely. Ben would have never gotten that job offer from the Dallas Morning News without all your escapades. Do his parents know how many cases you've solved with the police? You're a regular brain trust."

"They think Ben did it all. I was just the maiden who needed rescuing."

Mary whistled low. "That is so wrong. You were the force that found the murderers. I think my boss would hire you as a cop if you were ever interested. Which also brings me to the things you've done for my career. You're an amazing, if not significantly nosy, girl."

Mary's words were making me feel better. I *was* smart. Ben's parents made it sound like he was solely responsible for solving those crimes, but he wasn't. He helped, but it was mostly me and Mary.

I looked up at the belfry. "So, tell me what you have so far, and I'll tell you what I know."

Mary laughed and patted me on the back. "You betcha, partner."

"Want to go up there?" I asked, looking up toward the crime scene.

"I'm here in an unofficial capacity. I don't know how the department would feel about me going into the building." The department's acceptance of Mary was much better than it had been when she first joined the force, and no matter what happened, she was still there. But even though they now accepted her input on investigations, she never really trusted it would stay that way.

"Don't worry about it. I'm a bride, and I've made very few irrational demands. As far as I'm concerned, I'm due one," I assured her.

"So, I could follow you up there in the capacity of bridesmaid and not investigating officer?"

"Exactly." I grabbed her arm. "Come on. I know how to get up there now. Ben and I snuck up the other night."

"I don't even want to know why you and Ben were sneaking into the belfry," Mary said under her breath.

"It's not what you think. Well, for the most part, not what you think." We walked through the lobby, not making any noise. It was dark in the sanctuary except for the dim light that shone through the stained glass windows. Mary started looking on the wall for the light switch, but I stopped her.

"Don't," I whispered.

"I thought you said you were playing the demanding bride. If we're going to pull this off, we need to turn on the lights."

I wasn't as sure I could pull it off now that we were inside. If we turned on the lights, we would have to explain what we were doing and put on a show for the bride, who needed to see the belfry, but if we left them off, we could easily slip in and out, and no one would have to be accounted for.

"Let's just see if we can do this without anybody noticing, okay? My acting skills are not all that great."

"*Now* you tell me? Okay. You're the bride."

Once we shut the outer door, the bright light from the lobby only shone through a tiny gap between the door and floor. The air in the chapel was warm and heavy and reeked of lemon oil and beeswax candles. The wooden pews, lit only by the subtle colors of the sun coming through darkened stained glass, stood like sentinels before us, waiting for us to pass. The windowless altar stood shrouded in darkness.

The quietness of the sanctuary was haunting, and I found my gaze darting to the corners as if congregants from years past still existed in the stale air shut in by the stained glass windows.

"It's this way," I whispered, feeling for Mary's hand.

Mary crossed herself. "*En el nombre del Padre, y del Hijo y del Espíritu Santo. Amén.*"

"What was that for?"

"Protection. Let's walk." Mary whispered.

Chapter Eight

I stumbled on the first step up to the altar, causing a candle stand to wobble.

"Be careful," Mary said. "It would be pretty hard to explain if you broke something on the altar. Even crazy brides don't get to be that crazy."

Walking forward, the light from the stained glass didn't reflect in this area. I felt the outline of the organ and then the doorway that led to the belfry. The door was still unlocked, and upon opening it, the light from the belfry shone down, shedding light into the darkened altar area.

We ran up the stairs and out of the sanctuary so quickly that I worried we would be heard in one of the offices or rooms; the thumping of our footsteps was so loud. Our bodies curved around the staircase, and once at the top, we both gasped for breath.

The heat in the stairwell at midday was much heavier than it had been the evening Ben and I visited the belfry. I greedily breathed the clean air making its way through the openings in the bell frame.

"Okay, you got me up here," Mary said, still catching her breath. "Now what did you want to show me?"

"How much time did the police spend up here when they were investigating?" I asked.

"I don't know. Enough, I guess. Only a couple of people got to come up here. Detective Barrerra spent most of the time looking at the caretaker's body. Why?"

"When Ben and I were up here, I noticed a place in the dust where someone must have dragged Earl's body. That's when I first started to suspect that it was not an accident."

"I never thought it was. People don't fall like that if they are awake. I saw a jumper once in Houston. Except for the blood around the head, the person looked like they were sleeping. Maybe some people land that way, but I had just never seen anything like it."

"Assuming Earl was thrown over, whoever did this had to be strong enough to get him up and over the edge. How tall would you say that is?" I pointed to one of the open squares that framed the bell in the belfry.

"At least four feet. That's a steep climb to lift a body over," Mary said.

"So, it would have to be a man to do it."

"Or a very strong woman."

"Yes, I guess. Are there any women weightlifters on your suspect list?"

Mary rolled her eyes. "Gee, that's one question we forgot to ask."

I looked below at the church lawn where Earl had landed. Clarence was parking his car. In contrast to Vernice's jalopy, he drove a light green Volkswagen Bug that looked in perfect condition. Even though the sky had become partly cloudy, the paint on the Volkswagen gleamed in the light. Clarence pulled a large instrument case out of the back seat, locked the car, and headed into the church.

"Uh oh," I said, still looking out.

"What?" Mary was still staring at the path in the dust on the floor of the belfry.

"The choir director is coming into the church. There's a chance he might want to practice in the sanctuary, which means we'll have to explain to him why we snuck up here."

"I guess it's time for you to act like a bride. Get your pouty face ready," Mary joked. "Besides, it's getting hot up here."

"I guess I'll have to try. I did play Juliet in high school."

"And you're even hanging out in the belfry. That's pretty close to a balcony." Mary winked.

I wasn't sure Mary would think I was such a good actress once we tried to get past Clarence. "The choir director, Clarence, can be skeptical."

"I believe in you. One thing I've learned in this job is people you'd never expect can be excellent liars. You can lie with the best of them."

We started to leave, and something else occurred to me. "One more thing. When we were looking around up here, I found a part of a zipper."

"So?"

"It was a pull. You know, the part you pull the zipper up with. It was embedded into the side of the wall where we think Earl went over. I'd guess it was from a big zipper, from the size of it. My theory is, and it's just a theory, that it might have come off when whoever threw Earl over brushed against the wall."

Mary raised her chin slightly. "That's interesting. Do you still have it?"

"Yes. It's in my purse, but Ben has it right now at the rental house."

"Good. I'll need you to drop it by the station. I want to add it to the evidence. We don't have much at this point."

We made our way back down the creaky stairway. When we came out of the door, Clarence had just started playing a run of low notes on a bass fiddle that sounded like the backup to a jazz piece. He jumped when he saw us and dropped the bow he was using, causing the strings to twang and echo in the sanctuary.

"Oh my God. Where did you come from?"

"Sorry if we scared you. I wanted to see the belfry," I said.

"Heavens to Betsy, why?"

I put on my best moody bride face. "I just did. I know you probably don't understand this, but I want everything to be perfect, just perfect. We were just up there trying to get some peace after what happened to your poor caretaker. It's such an awful shame."

Mary nodded. "Awful shame."

Clarence gave a perfunctory nod. "Yes, indeed it is. May he rest in peace." He took a beat and then said, "While Earl was well-liked and a valued volunteer of our congregation, it might surprise you to know that not everyone in the church appreciated Earl's sense of morality."

"Morality? Isn't that like the lifeblood of a church? I thought that was the point," Mary said.

"Of course, everyone should practice good habits, but Earl had a way of uncovering the embarrassing foibles of people in our congregation. Once he knew something about somebody, there would be no peace until that person put right whatever it was. It could be embarrassing for that person. Things are not always black and white, you know. But to Earl, they were. It makes me wonder about him."

"Did Earl ever accuse you of anything?" I asked.

Clarence put a hand to his thin neck. "No. It would be hard to find me doing anything immoral. I'm way too boring for that. I know we musicians have a reputation for imbibing in drugs and alcohol, but I was never that type. I spent my life in a continual stream of music lessons and practicing, but our beloved caretaker did go after a person I like to think of as a friend. I can only hope she would say the same about me."

"And who was this friend?" I asked.

Clarence's lips tightened. "If I told you that, I would have to tell you what he was accusing her of, and at this time, I choose to protect her privacy. It's the gentlemanly thing to do." He nodded primly.

"Of course," Mary said. "There aren't enough gentlemen out there these days. I'm sure she appreciates your willingness to keep her secrets."

"Thank you for understanding, not that it's any of your business. Now, if you'll excuse me, I need to practice. The acoustics in this room are perfect."

"Yes, of course," I said. "Are you practicing for one of your gigs in Dallas?"

Clarence brightened. "As a matter of fact, I am. We just got booked in the Elk's club, and they like their jazz cool and clean."

"Groovy," said Mary.

Clarence nodded and resumed the music he had been working on when we surprised him.

Once we closed the door to the sanctuary, I whispered, "I wonder who he's covering for?"

"Whoever it is," Mary said in a low voice, "I would bet he has a giant crush on her."

Chapter Nine

Vernice and I met the next day in the church kitchen to go over the food list for the reception. The kitchen looked like any other kitchen, except everything was bigger. There was a sturdy double farm sink, as well as a beaten-up off-white stove with gas burners. The linoleum floor was scuffed as if someone had dropped a soup pan or two. All the countertops were Formica as well, with a faded speckled pattern running through them. The table we sat at had a red gingham tablecloth, which shone under the fluorescent tube lighting fixture that hung over us. There was a lingering smell of onions, laced with kitchen disinfectants.

As we sat at the table, me with my notebook and Vernice with a large yellow legal pad, she began to go through the food list and the people who would be cooking for us. Vernice had a standard menu she used for all the weddings she oversaw. It included roast chicken, potatoes, green beans, and fluffy yeast rolls, all made by the ladies of Camden Chapel. We only had to pay the cost of the food. A lady from the church volunteered to make the wedding cake. Like the executive chef at the Ritz, Vernice rattled off information about time schedules and keeping food hot. With that amount of detail, it was then I realized she would have a good idea who might have hated Earl enough to give him tranquilizers and toss him off the belfry of his beloved Camden Chapel.

"So, the roast chicken will have to come out of the oven just as you are saying your I do's..."

I wrote everything she said down in my notebook, and she beamed with happiness at how seriously I took my role and documented her efforts.

"Would you mind terribly if I borrowed your little notebook for a day? It's genius how you put it together, and I would like to create one of my own. I could use it as a template for future brides."

I pitied the next doe-eyed bride who would find herself immersed in the endless lists Vernice would give to her. "Uh, sure, I don't think I'm going to need it in the next couple of days. We're so close, there's very little planning left to do." I handed her the notebook, although I immediately felt naked without it.

"Terrific. I'll use it as a template to create my own version of what you have here, and then have the church stock the notebooks in the supplies closet—"

Before she could continue with all the details of her plan, I interrupted. "Uh, Vernice, can I ask you something?"

She looked pleasantly surprised. Although she had encouraged me to share my worries and concerns with her, promising absolute confidentiality in an effort to build a stronger friendship, I still hadn't confided in her as she had hoped. She was smiling now, but I wasn't sure how she would feel when she realized I was digging for information about Earl. "Of course, my dear. Anything."

"Thank you. It's just that this thing with Earl is really bugging me. I was wondering how he got along with everyone here at the church. He seemed like such a nice man to me, but I only met him once."

Vernice put her elbows on the table and then rested her chin on her hands. She looked a little disappointed I hadn't asked her anything about married life, but she let out an exasperated sigh and began talking. "Well, Earl was a lovely man, that's for sure."

Her tone led me to believe there was more to her story. "But?" I asked, trying to prompt her to share the information I really wanted.

"But, when people work together day after day, even people who profess to be a part of a forgiving community, they can get on each other's nerves. Not me, of course. Earl and I got along great, but last week I did walk in on a little argument."

"Who was he arguing with?"

Looking around the room, her eyes darted to the doorway before settling back on me. She leaned forward to whisper her secret. "Davita Ross. I don't know what she was upset about, but you know how Davita can be." She gave me a knowing wink, as if I actually knew how Davita could be. "When I walked in, she was telling him to mind his own damn business."

My eyes widened. "She said that?"

"Yes, I know. You'd think a pastor's wife would not have that kind of a potty mouth, but yes." She held a hand up. "With God as my witness, that's what I heard."

"What happened then?"

"They saw me and stopped talking. Davita stormed off, and all Earl said was that he had to cut the grass."

"So, you don't have any idea what they were arguing about?"

"No, but Davita was plenty hot under the collar, that's for sure."

"The person I least suspected you would bring up would be the pastor's wife."

"Yes. Davita constantly surprises us. Old Pastor Treadwell, you never met him, his wife, Dorothy, was as sweet as could be. You'd never catch her arguing with a member of the congregation."

I interrupted Vernice before she launched into the unabridged history of Camden Chapel. "Do you know anyone else who might have quarreled with Earl?"

"Why are you asking all these questions? I didn't answer right away, which piqued Vernice's interest. "Earl's fall was an accident."

She wasn't dumb, and I didn't know if the police had released the information about Earl being drugged. If I let Vernice know about the tranquilizers, I might endanger Mary's job. I tried to sound casual.

"Yes, of course. A terrible accident. I was curious, that's all."

Once I convinced her I wasn't holding anything back, she gave a patronizing little smile and nodded. "You're so young." She looked up in thought, and then her gaze met mine. "I don't think Clarence liked him, but then Clarence is such an odd bird. He talks on and on about that trio he plays in. He acts like he is a big-time performer, like he's on the Lawrence Welk show or something. A choir director is just a choir director, I always say. I have to think Earl might have thought the same and made a try at putting Clarence in his place."

I stayed quiet, not wanting to agree with her insulting comments. Even though Clarence was a bit quirky, I didn't dislike him. She didn't notice my silence, which was good, because in my head I was making a list.

Number one would be Davita. Number two might just be Clarence.

The sweet, grandfatherly man I met clearly had more to him than selflessly taking care of the Camden Chapel. He was trying to fix people's lives along with the lightbulbs.

Once Vernice and I talked through the menu, she looked at her watch. "Sorry to cut this short, Dot, but I need to get home and do some cleaning before Eddie gets back. He likes our house to be spotless, and I love making him happy."

"Oh, sure." I tried to sound disappointed at her bringing our meeting to a close, but it couldn't be further from the truth.

"Try to decide on your music, dear. Davita's good, but probably not the caliber where you could hand her sheet music on your way up the aisle." She picked up the bridal notebook and gave a little wave. "You can follow me out."

I picked up my things and obediently followed Vernice out, noticing the bright orange flowers on her dress seemed to be dancing back and forth as her behind wobbled when she walked. As we reached the lobby, Pastor Ross was just coming out of his office.

"Vernice," he said. "Glad I caught you. I got a call this morning from Eunice Michaels. I guess their oldest son is getting married in November. You remember him, don't you? Forrest?"

Vernice scrunched her mouth to one side as she thought. "Is that the boy who went to college to study oil wells?"

"Very good. Yes, he got a degree in oil and gas management. Do you think we could get together after Dot's wedding and get the ball rolling on that one?"

Vernice puffed out her chest like a rooster. "Wonderful. Of course. It seems all our little chicks are getting married, first Ben Dalton and now

Forrest Michaels. It's wonderful. Just wonderful." She turned to me. "Have to run. Ta-Ta!"

"She sure gets excited about wedding planning," I said, as Vernice closed the outer door.

"She does, and I don't know what we'd do without her. I'm not good at putting things like that together, and Davita, well. Let's just say, she's busy with other things."

"Yes. I'm so glad she will be singing for the wedding, but I'm afraid I still haven't given her the song."

"That's okay," the pastor said. "There's been a lot going on around here. I'm finding it hard to write my sermon for this week. I'm going to have to talk about our loss, but I just don't know where to begin."

"Were you and Earl good friends?"

Pastor Ross put a hand to his chin, rubbing it across dark brown stubble. "Yes and no. Like Vernice, his services to our church were invaluable. I can do a few things around the house, but nothing like what Earl could do. But he contributed so much more. He was driven to fix things. Some days, he was here longer than I was. Sometimes people spend a lot of time in fellowship at church because this is where their family is. Not their flesh and blood family, but their chosen family. We all come together because of the love of God, and that seems to envelop everyone. Well, except for church council meetings, where we argue over the color of the new carpet. That can't be helped. Everyone had a place in their heart for our Earl."

This was a side of Earl and the people of Camden Chapel I hadn't seen before. It went from a group of nosy, cliquish people to united members of a congregation who spent time together and, like a family, cared about each other to the point of interference on occasion.

"Did you know anyone who didn't like Earl?"

Pastor Ross laughed. "A few. He had a way of getting under people's skin. My own wife said a few choice things about him." After saying that, he cleared his throat, as if he had gone too far.

"Vernice has said a few things, too," I added.

"No doubt."

"How about you? Did you ever disagree with Earl?"

He shrugged. "I'm the pastor. It's my job to keep my grievances to myself. For the most part, we got along. The man was dedicating his life to making the church look beautiful. How could I dislike that?"

"What will you do now?"

"I guess I need to turn to the Yellow Pages and start hiring people. Lord knows what this will do to the church budget." He stopped. "What am I saying? Our biggest loss is brother Earl, not the things he did for us. God will provide."

"I think it's a little of both." This conversation had gotten very interesting, especially the part about Davita going round with Earl about something. "Would it be okay if I stopped in at the parsonage and visited Davita? I have a question about the music."

He looked out the window in the direction of the parsonage next door. "Sure. She's home right now."

"Thank you," I said. "And I'm sorry for your loss."

"Thank you," he said in a whisper. "You know, nobody ever says that to me."

"They should, then."

Chapter Ten

After I finished up with Pastor Ross, finding Davita was not difficult. They lived in a house right next to the church that Ben called the parsonage. The sound of singing drifted over when I stepped out of the church. The windows of the parsonage were all open, and white lace curtains drifted in and out of the window frames, bumping up against the screens, as if they were trying to find a way to circulate the air all on their own.

Davita's voice was strong and clear, but the music she was singing was nothing like "Ave Maria." She was singing a sultry version of Billie Holiday's "Body and Soul." Unless she had an accompanist in there with her, she was playing the piano and singing at the same time. She was not only beautiful but also talented. Davita didn't fit the stereotype of the normal pastor's wife who dished up warm casseroles and advice. There was something different about her, and it came through in her voice. A longing. I walked down the sidewalk that joined the parsonage to the church and knocked on the door.

The piano music stopped, as did the singing. A minute later, Davita opened the door wearing a yellow sundress and holding what looked like a glass of lemonade.

"Dot." She looked surprised to see me. "Have you finally decided which song you want me to sing?"

I still hadn't chosen anything. The pastor had suggested "What Wondrous Love is This," a traditional hymn, but I preferred a popular love song from the radio. My mother told me it was best to stay traditional, at least during the ceremony. "I don't yet. I'm sorry. I promise to have it to you soon. But I was wondering if I could talk to you for just a few minutes."

She stepped back. "Sure. Come on in. If you've come to ask me advice about marriage, I'm afraid you've got the wrong girl."

That was interesting. Vernice couldn't stop handing out free advice. The other day, she gave me a long lecture about how I shouldn't hang my "unmentionables" in the bathroom. Husbands like everything tidy and in its place. Davita seemed to be the opposite. "Well, no, that isn't the reason for my visit, but looking from this side, your marriage looks very successful."

"Yeah, I guess it does. The pastor and I are very good at putting up a united front, but that's not why you're here. How can I help? Would you like some water or lemonade?"

"I would love a glass of water. It's so hot."

"I know. This Texas heat is going to kill me one day." She went into the kitchen and returned with a sparkling glass. I sat down on a slightly worn avocado green couch. There was a doily on a polished coffee table, and a picture of Jesus hung on the wall along with a collection of crosses scattered about. A black phone sat on a side table near the door, and I could imagine Pastor Ross getting a late-night call from a parishioner in crisis and grabbing a coat off the coat tree that stood beside it.

I took an unladylike gulp of the cool liquid. "Thank you for the drink. This wedding planning is tougher than I thought."

She sat across from me in a floral wingback chair. "Yes, but with Vernice you'll come out all right. She's handled dozens of weddings."

I wasn't sure if I could smoothly segue into my true reason for the visit. From what Vernice had told me, Earl wasn't Davita's favorite church volunteer. How would she react if she knew I had talked to two people who confided in me about her disagreement with him? I decided to just jump in. "I know. Actually, the reason I've come here today has more to do with Earl."

"Earl?" She cocked her head to one side.

"Yes. I was told that you had an argument with him before he died."

A transformation came over Davita, and her pleasant smile disappeared. Even though it was warm, I felt a sudden chill in the room. "Who told you that?"

"I'd rather not say." I didn't want to get anyone in trouble. If this church really did operate as a big family, this would be bad for anyone who went against the pastor's wife. "Is it true?"

"I think I know who told you. It was Vernice, wasn't it? That woman is a busybody." Her tone was harsh, and she took a drink of her lemonade that I was beginning to think wasn't lemonade. "Yes, we had an argument, but it has nothing to do with him jumping out of the belfry. That man had a problem minding his own business, and—news for you—I wasn't the only one whose business he felt a right to get into. I've never met a woman who meddled the way he did."

Again, I chose to keep the information about the tranquilizers to myself. "May I ask what you were arguing about?"

She scowled. "I hardly think it's any of your business. Something you need to know about a church. You can overhear a lot of things you shouldn't. Sanctuaries are like echo chambers. That old man had a way of showing up at just the wrong time. He told Roger he was always fixing things, but what he was really doing was hanging out in the shadows, trying to get dirt on folks. He was a first-class creeper."

"And that's what he did? He surprised you?"

She shook her head back and forth quickly, signifying a 'no.' "He surprised everyone. That's the problem with living in a little town. Everyone knows your business. Did you know that before I married Roger, I used to sing at the Silk Club in Dallas?"

"No. I didn't. I've never heard of it. But I can believe it. I heard you singing when I came up the walk. You have a beautiful voice, like Judy Garland. I hope Camden Chapel lets you sing. So, was the Silk Club a theater or a supper club?"

She seemed to warm slightly at my compliment. "More like a supper club. People loved me. People drove from one-stoplight places like this to hear me." Her eyes were no longer focused on me. She looked out the window as if the Silk Club was just outside the lace curtains.

"Why did you stop?" I asked.

That broke her concentration. "I stopped to get married."

"But then you didn't start back working after you got married? It seems like such a shame."

"I married a pastor. The pastor's wife never works. That's an unwritten rule." Her tone was bitter. "Earl found something of mine hidden behind the organ pipes." She placed her lemonade on a coaster that had a mosaic cross made out of different colors of cork, then she quietly folded her hands in her lap.

"What did he find?" I asked.

"If you must know, in a moment of despair, I packed a suitcase. I was planning to run off to Dallas and go back into the business. You can't understand how much I missed hearing the audience clap after I sang. I never went through with leaving, but Earl found the bag and threatened to tell my husband. I think he was protecting him from me. Clarence knew about it, too, but he thought it was a great idea. He understood how incomplete I felt, and he promised not to tell. Either way, I snuck it back to the house and unpacked my clothes. Roger never knew."

Her words shook me. She was a living example of what I most feared. Being pigeonholed and unable to pursue what you want to do. "You know, I think I'm discovering that me working is not what Ben's family wants."

She blew out a sigh. "Stand your ground. I wish I had."

"I'm trying, but it's hard. I'm not sure, but I think Ben wants me to be a housewife, too. He's never acted like he wants me to stay home once we're married. As a matter of fact, I always thought he liked my independence."

"Sure, they find it attractive at first, but then once you're married, things can change. You need to talk to Ben. Straighten it out now, or you'll be hiding a suitcase, making plans that don't include him."

I knew she was right. I would talk to Ben. This is what someone in a healthy marriage would do, right? Talking out things you disagree on before they get any bigger. I turned to Davita. "Thanks for talking to me, and thanks for the water."

"Of course."

I started to go and then turned around. "You never should have stopped singing, even if you are a pastor's wife. You have a beautiful voice."

Her lips trembled into a little smile. "Thanks, kid."

Chapter Eleven

When I returned to the apartment, the ringing of the phone echoed against the rapidly emptying walls.

"Dot? This is Leslie Dalton, your future mother-in-law. That sounds funny, doesn't it? I never thought about being a mother-in-law. I guess I expected Ben to marry, but forgot about that part."

"Hi, Mrs. Dalton," I answered, still out of breath. "How are you?" I wondered if she had called Ben with more wedding questions, and he had directed her to me. It might be a good start after our dinner at their house.

"Please, call me Leslie. I wanted to invite you to our ladies' luncheon after church tomorrow."

"Ladies' luncheon?" I asked.

"Yes. The ladies of our church get together once a month, and well, since you'll soon be a new member, I thought this would be a great way for you to get to know some of the other women at the church."

Ben and I had never discussed joining his family's church. Now it seemed to be an assumption. My family went to a Methodist church in town, where, although the services were not all that different from Camden Chapel, it should be one of the options when Ben and I were deciding where to attend as a couple. Honestly, neither Ben nor I had attended church regularly in a while, even before we began dating. His mother had to know that, so it was a little discomforting that she was assuming that not only was her only son getting married, but being there for our wedding would light a fire in him, and he'd be dying to go back. You would think with all the life and death situations Ben and I had encountered together, we would have discussed our beliefs, but we hadn't. I suddenly had the urge to call him and get his take on his mother's assumption.

"The ladies really are a lovely bunch," she said. "Whether you need a recipe or just a shoulder to cry on, they'll be there for you. I don't know what I would have done without my friendships at church."

"That's really nice to hear. Um, if you don't mind, let me check with Ben. When and where is the lunch exactly?"

"It's right after church in the fellowship hall. Oh, I hope you can make it."

It was a sweet gesture, and I decided attending was a good idea. Even though I said I wanted to talk to Ben, I dialed up Ellie first.

"It's just a lunch, Dot," Ellie said. I heard the sound of the cash register in the background. I could picture her as I had seen her many times, standing in front of the register with the phone crooked to her ear and the long black cord winding behind her.

"Don't you understand? It's so much more than that. She thinks we are joining the church. I don't mind going to the luncheon, but where does this go from there?"

"Are you thinking about joining the church? Al's family is Catholic, and we've discussed attending mass once Al, Jr. is born."

For some reason, this simple question unnerved me. "I don't know. I hadn't thought about it."

"Dot, I can't help thinking you're getting all wound up for nothing. If you have a problem with the way you think this is going, then tell Ben's mom that. What does Ben say?"

I let out a moan. "I don't know that either. I was about to call him."

"There's your first step."

"I know. When you got married, were your or Al's parents making assumptions about you?"

Ellie laughed. "My mother was so happy I was marrying somebody, anybody, she would have jumped through fire to pull it off. Al's mom is all he has left, and she lives in Florida, so all she did was show up after we got married. I guess it was pretty easy for me."

"Not for me."

"I know your parents belong to the Methodist church. With all you have going on right now, this seems like a minor thing you can work out once you get married. Also, once you figure out this caretaker thing. Don't deny it. I know you are quietly working the case." She had a point there. You can't fool Ellie, so don't even try. Just one of the things I like about her.

"So, will there be some of those delicious casseroles church ladies are notorious for?" I could sense my eight-months-pregnant cousin salivating on the other end.

"I would think so."

"Well then, if you need a sidekick or moral support, I'd love to go with you. I never met a casserole I didn't like. You think they'll have some pickles on the side?"

"Really? You want to come with me? I could hug you right now. Yes! I need a sidekick."

"Ha. Your sidekick gets kicks in her side all the time right now. Get it?"

"I get it. A pregnant joke. You should go on the road with that material. Hey, thank you, Ellie."

"What are cousins for?"

I hung up and felt better about everything. I needed to stay calm. The closer we got to the wedding, the more I panicked about things that didn't warrant it. I dialed Ben at the newspaper. Based on the amount of key clacking I heard in the background, he sounded busy.

"What's up, Dot?"

"Your mother just called and wants me to go to the ladies' lunch after church."

"Okay. You should go. It ought to be fun. What's the problem?"

"Ben." I tried to keep the exasperation out of my voice. "She's thinking that we are joining the church now as a married couple."

"Hmmm." More key clicking. I wasn't even sure if he knew what we were talking about. How long would he go on typing before realizing he should be talking to me?

"Ben!"

"What?"

"So, are we joining the church?"

There was a pause and then, "I don't know. I hadn't thought about it. I don't go to church now, but I suppose…." He went back to tapping.

"You suppose what? Honestly, Ben Dalton, this is not the kind of thing you just let happen. We need to talk about this."

"Uh, Dot. I've got to go. Can we talk about it tonight?"

"Sure." The phone clicked off on his side.

All of a sudden, I realized that I was becoming a part of another family. I wasn't ready for that yet. I looked at my watch. It was Saturday afternoon, and my mother and father would be at home doing weekly chores. My mother cleaned the house while my father worked on the cars and anything that needed repairing. I used to be a part of this weekly ritual helping both my mother and my father. I could be doing anything from changing the oil in his car or dusting the knick-knacks in the front room.

I pulled up to my childhood home and could hear the vacuum cleaner winding its way through the house. I opened the door and called out my mother's name. My dad was coming up from his basement workshop, holding a sprinkler in his hand.

"Hello, Dot! We didn't expect you today." He yelled over the sound of the vacuum. "I'm afraid we're pretty busy getting the house ready for the wedding. You know your Uncle George is coming in with your Grandma Morgan."

"Yes."

The vacuum cleaner cut off. "Do I hear Dot?" my mother said from the other room.

"Yes, sorry. I should have called."

She came out dragging the vacuum cleaner behind her. "You never have to call. You live here. Or you did. This is your home. Locks and phone calls are not for you."

She had no idea how happy I was to be reminded I was always welcome in this place.

"What brings you over, Dot? Is there a problem with the wedding? Did the church cancel it because of the accident?" My dad set the sprinkler on the table.

"No, they are still planning on hosting the wedding, but I did want to get your opinion on something."

As if they'd heard a cue from off stage, both parents went to the kitchen and took a chair.

"Sure. We'll do our best." My mother looked concerned.

"Okay." I pulled up my own chair. It was funny that after all these years, we each took the seats we had always sat in for breakfast, lunch, and dinner. That gave me a sense of comfort after all the new things I was encountering.

"I'm getting the feeling that Ben's parents expect us to join his church."

My dad grew closer. "Did they ask you if you wanted to join?"

"No. That's the thing. They have all these ideas of what church we will go to, how long before we have a baby, and even if I should work."

"Why is it their decision?" my mom asked. "Surely, they know you and Ben are adults."

"You would think so."

"I know. This is a lot for parents when their kids get married. We're struggling with it," Mom said.

"You are?" I asked.

My mom tapped her fingers on the table. "Just a little. You're our little girl, after all. We're also a little jealous you will have a second set of parents who will be guiding you. The church decision proves that."

Dad cleared his throat. "You know, they must be struggling with the same things about Ben that we are with you, plus things are tense over at their church with Earl Gunther's death. I've been meaning to tell you that I saw Earl in court last year."

"I didn't know that. Why was he in court?"

"Oh, it was all pretty silly in the end. He got into an argument with a neighbor because the city allows one trash can at the curb. The neighbor was putting two out, and so Dinty, the trash pickup guy, would take the two together and leave Earl's can. We were never totally sure if he really didn't see Earl's can or if it was just easier to pick up the two that were close together. He told the judge he thought he had two houses and two cans."

"I'll bet that judge who studied law all those years never thought he'd be spending his time settling trash disputes," Mom said. "I just baked a batch of my peanut butter cookies. Would you like one?"

"That would be great. Thanks, Mom." She left the table and pulled a Tupperware container off the counter, then handed me one. This moment between the three of us was just like thousands of others, but somehow it was also different. We would never be the same after I married. "Uh, Mom, I just wanted to say thank you."

As she gave a cookie to Dad and then took one for herself, she looked confused. "I think you already did that, dear."

"No. Thanks for being my mom and giving me such a wonderful home to grow up in."

She sat down slowly. "Dot, is everything okay? Between you and Ben? You aren't having second thoughts about this wedding, are you?"

"Pumpkin, it's a big decision, and nobody would fault you if you needed more time," my dad said.

If it were only that easy. "I don't think so, Dad. It's just—" I felt my throat closing up. "It's just so much to take on. I'm not just marrying Ben, but I'm marrying his family, and unexpectedly, I have a bunch of church ladies who want to have lunch with me."

Mom laughed. "Oh God, you are in trouble." Then we all laughed.

Dad spoke in the gentle way I loved. "Dot, you're looking too far ahead. Just take it day by day. That's all anyone can do, and if there is something happening you feel isn't what you want, say something. Be kind, and polite, but say something."

My dad would put that last part on. He always stressed communicating now to fend off troubles later.

"You're right. One day at a time."

"Yep. It's as simple as that." Dad stood up. "Now, unless you're planning on helping around here, I need to get back to work." He started to go and then turned around. "I will tell you one thing I heard. Earl was down at Gleason's Hardware last week, and he snapped at Carlton. He then apologized and said he had something on his mind."

I looked at my father. "Did he say what it was?"

"That's the thing. He wouldn't tell Carlton any of the details, just that he felt like he was back on patrol and had come across a very unsavory situation."

"You mean like whatever it was, someone was probably breaking the law?"

My dad shrugged his shoulders. "Maybe. It sounds like his idea of law-breaking might be a lot of things. That Earl was a straight arrow."

I picked up my bag. "I wish he had said more. In the meantime, I'm going to get going before someone hands me a broom."

Chapter Twelve

"There you are, dear girl." Leslie Dalton stood from where she had been seated at a long table as I walked in, holding a bag of rolls from the bakery. I had been informed through Ben that my job was to bring some rolls to add to the potluck fare. I didn't have the time or the energy to cook anything between the wedding and the never-ending questions rolling through my mind about the death of Earl Gunther.

"So glad you made it." She looked behind me. She was still dressed in her church finery, a white suit with navy trim, and white pumps that sported a navy toe section. I had dug out a dark red sleeveless shift with white piping that crisscrossed in the front under a high collar. I bought the dress last year when I was working at the funeral home and was told to wear only dark colors. Leslie held her palm upward. "It feels like rain out there. So stuffy. You can put the rolls over there. I pulled an empty bread basket out of the church kitchen for you. In a way, this kitchen belongs to all the women here at Camden Chapel. So much of our social activities revolve around it. Look around and make yourself at home."

My future mother-in-law's voice was animated. This was her world, and she was clearly in her element. There were four long tables that had been pushed into a square surrounded by chatting women of all ages. A few looked over and smiled, and one even gave a small finger wave. The scents of April in Paris, Shalimar, and Chanel Number Five drifted around me. It was like visiting a big department store in Dallas.

"Where do I sit?" I asked as I placed the rolls into the basket and added it to a serving table next to other rolls. I looked around the room for Vernice, who would undoubtedly come sit by me with a fresh list of duties to do before the wedding. "Where's Vernice?"

"Oh, she went home right after church. Something about getting her house ready before the boys come home from camp." She put a hand on her chin and, with a twinkle in her eye, said, "I think you should find an empty seat and try to get to know one of our ladies. Who knows, you might be starting a lifelong friendship. Pick anyone."

"You don't want me to sit with you? Ben told me you were worried about some wedding details. I thought you might want to go over them with me."

"Sweet Dot. No. No. This is your wedding, and whatever you plan, we'll live with it and be happy about it. You have the rest of your life to sit with me. This is a friend-finding adventure." She let out a little giggle, sounding proud of her title for my mission.

"Okay," I said. Looking around, most of the ladies were standing in little clusters talking. There were a few pastel hats with feathers sticking out, and a couple of the ladies wore white gloves. I was guessing fried chicken was not on the menu. Charlotte, the organist, was sitting by herself on the side, and as I glanced at her, she raised a hand, motioning me to come over.

"Please come sit by me. Don't let me get surrounded by the menopause queens," she said.

I stifled a laugh, hoping my future mother-in-law didn't hear what Charlotte had said. She was right. The average age at the luncheon was over fifty.

"Thank God you're here. I've only been working here a while, but it seems like this congregation is aging every time I look out over the organ. Wherever you look, it's old, older, or real real old."

I was surprised, but I found Charlotte to be actually very funny. She had the guts to say the things I was thinking, and I liked that about her. She wore her brown hair in what was called a flip. Straight all the way down to her neck, and then it flipped up into one curl that encircled her head. I had seen Marlo Thomas wear her hair that way in the ads for the new show coming in September, *That Girl.*

"So, are you ready for the wedding?" Charlotte asked.

"No. But is anyone ever? I've been to a dozen weddings but never knew just how many things have to be done to pull them off."

"I wouldn't know. I've never been married myself, although I have been engaged to Mac for almost five years."

"Five years. That's a long engagement."

"Tell me about it. If it were my decision, we'd be married with a couple of kids by now, but Mac is the king of cold feet. He's a little younger than I am, and, well, you know men. He lives in the moment and the future; he wants to be sure."

"I think I'm experiencing a little of that myself. Now that we're so close to the wedding, I thought I'd be surer about everything."

Charlotte looked surprised. "No. Seriously? That groom of yours is quite the looker, if I say so myself. With Mac, I think he feels like we're great together, but he keeps stalling. I guess that old thing about giving the milk away will never sell the cow is true. Oh well, but you'd be a fool to let that sweet man get away."

"I agree. It's just a lot, you know. All the wedding stuff, then your caretaker has an accident and falls out of the belfry. Vernice tells me pre-wedding jitters are normal. Thank God I have her helping me. When Ben's mother suggested using her, I didn't know, but now she's a lifesaver. She knows everything about everything."

Charlotte sat back and smirked. "Is that what she told you?"

"Of course." Charlotte's implied opinion was obvious. Even though I was praising Vernice, there was a downside. Vernice bragged about having her finger on the pulse of all things. She knew just who to call for anything that might come up, but we had to push to get her to use Lily for the flowers. She liked everything done a certain way. Her way. At first, it was reassuring there was someone who knew the ins and outs of wedding planning, but eventually she became annoying. I was always doing things not quite right for her.

Charlotte drew closer. "Vernice doesn't know anything about anything. You know how she's always touting the virtues of that Eddie? Her perfect husband? I've got news for you. If you ask me, Eddie's a rat. Why does he need to take all those trips to Dallas for business? Eddie sells construction equipment. Now I know Dallas is booming, but just how many excavators do they need? Why doesn't he ever go to Houston or San Antonio, or even little Austin? Perfect Eddie is cheating on her. I'd bet my life on it."

The thought of Eddie being unfaithful bothered me. Just meeting Lily, a woman from Ben's past, made me downright squeamish. "Come on. That can't be true. Vernice seems very happy in her marriage. I was hoping mine would be as loving."

Charlotte looked side to side, making sure there were no ladies listening. "Yeah, well, I saw Eddie flirting with the pastor's wife a few weeks ago. He was dishing it out, and she was eating it up. He's a romancer, I tell you. I've seen guys like Eddie before. He thinks he's Frankie Avalon, and the rest of the females in the world are Annette Funicello hanging on his every word while sticking out her C cups. The funniest part of all is that Vernice doesn't seem to have an inkling about what's going on."

Listening to Charlotte tell me about a skeleton in the closet in Vernice's life made me question the front she put up. This was one of those times when the person you meet is not all she seems. It didn't do much for me as far as trusting her with my big day.

My cousin Ellie came in, out of breath, and sat down in the chair next to me. "Oh, sorry, I'm late. I meant to be here on time this time, but the August weddings are keeping me busy."

Charlotte's face changed immediately into a wide smile. "And a baby on the way to boot. You're an amazing woman. When is the baby due, anyway?"

"Not until early September, but it feels like it's warming up for an early arrival. The baby has already dropped."

"What does that mean? Is he okay?" I asked.

Charlotte answered before Ellie could. "Basically, the baby's head is down. Kind of like a plane approaching a runway, if you know what I mean."

Relief filled me. The closer we got to this baby's delivery day, the more I worried about how everything would go. "Oh, I get it. That's very exciting. Did you feel it when it dropped? Does this mean the baby could come any day?"

"I hope not. I haven't even packed my bag for the hospital yet." She looked at Charlotte. "How do you know about babies dropping?"

Charlotte straightened a flower in the centerpiece placed in front of us. "I used to be a nurse. Your long, hot summer is almost over. Sounds like the baby is close to coming."

"Thank goodness," Ellie said. "When we plan for the next one, you better bet I'll be delivering in January, not September. This heat is crazy enough, but when you add carrying a baby, it's miserable. Al is a saint for putting up with me."

Her words reminded me of Vernice's constant praise of her husband, Eddie. If, like Charlotte said, Eddie's flirting was noticed, had Ellie heard anything about him? "Ellie, you've worked with Vernice, right?"

"Oh yes. Vernice Schaeffer. The woman who loves to call ten times for something that can be settled in one call. She's famous among us folks who work weddings."

"That doesn't sound promising," I said.

"It's just that she can be a bit picky. We had a flower girl whose dress didn't fit because her mother couldn't be bothered to bring her in for a second fitting. I measured the little girl in the fall, but in the spring, just like flowers, little kids grow. Vernice had a fit, and I spent an evening sewing up a simpler version of the dress that would match the bridesmaids."

"Wow. She seemed so nice."

"See! I told you that Vernice is not all she claims to be," Charlotte said. "I saw her in a big old argument with Earl the other day."

"What were they arguing about?" I asked.

"I'm not really sure except that she told Earl he would be better off minding his own business. That was the thing with him. He always had his nose in other people's problems. He was always around some corner painting, fixing a door, or changing a light bulb. I think he was privy to more secrets than the pastor."

"That is really interesting."

Someone tinkled a glass near the front.

"Excuse me, ladies." The pastor stood with his hands steepled in front of him, waiting for the crowd to quiet down. "I'm sorry to interrupt your fellowship time, but I thought you'd like to know the police have changed their focus on Earl Gunther's death. He was well-loved around here, and this is even more saddening." He lowered his hands. "They found evidence of tranquilizers in his stomach. There is a good chance that our Earl was murdered, presumably drugged, and then pushed off the belfry."

A chorus of gasps went up around the room, and Ellie uttered, "Damn," under her breath.

"We will be having a prayer service tonight in the sanctuary to pray for Earl's family, the police, and lastly, the poor soul who did this to him." Pastor Ross put his hands in the praying position. "If we could have a moment of prayer."

Chapter Thirteen

That night, Ben and I held candles in the darkened sanctuary of Camden Chapel while the organ played "Softly and Tenderly, Jesus is Calling" in the background. The congregation sat holding their candles, some of them cupping the flame to prevent it from going out under the fans placed near the front to circulate the air. A mother with small children held a candle while her husband held a sleeping child, his head resting on a broad shoulder.

Earl's wife, Maureen, sat in the front row along with a woman who was slightly hunched over. That had to be his mother. I couldn't imagine how sad it would be to outlive a child.

Even though the sanctuary was filled, there was a quiet reverence, most people choosing not to talk. The silence was broken when Vernice bustled in next to us in a black and white floral dress. She set her bag and an unlit candle next to us on the pew and whispered a thank you.

"Just look at them up there." She bent her head toward the first pew. "So very sad. One day you have a husband and the next day, poof, he's gone. I don't know what I would do if that ever happened to me. Of course, my Eddie is very careful and wouldn't dream of going on the roof. He has me call people for things like that." Even though no one was singing, possibly out of habit, Vernice nodded and pulled a hymnal out of the wooden rack built into the back of the pew. I heard an audible "Hmmm" as she pulled a folded piece of paper out of the back of the red leather book. "Some people do not have the common courtesy to throw away their bulletin after church."

She whispered, "It's a regular Easter egg hunt in here some Sunday afternoons." She unfolded the paper, and a look of confusion came over her features. "This is strange."

I held my candle close to the unfolded scrap she was holding up. From what I could make out in the semi-darkness, what she was holding was not a bulletin but a list of some sort. She lifted the paper slightly so we could read the words. "What do you make of this?"

- 8-3 work
- 3. Home Alone
- 7-4 work
- Lunch at diner

It didn't seem important, but I nudged Ben. "What do you think this is?"

Ben squinted and moved his lit candle closer, doubling our light on the handwriting. "It looks like someone's work schedule. Maybe they were counting hours for a paycheck."

Vernice took it back. "You're right. That has to be it. I should have known with your reporter skills you'd figure it out. Still, I'm going to have a think on this. Maybe someone else in the church knows. This could be important to someone in the congregation. We might even have the pastor hold it up after church and ask if anyone is missing their work hours."

As she finished her words, there was a shush from behind us, and she folded the paper back up and put it in her bag. As she lit her own candle from mine, Ben's mother and father came down the aisle and stood before our pew. Leslie gave Vernice a look.

"Could you scoot down just a bit?" Ben's mother said, cocking her head to the side.

"Oh, of course." We all began scooting, and Ben's parents squeezed in next to me, making a fully filled pew.

"Sorry we're late," Leslie said. She smelled of Shalimar, probably a fresh spray before church. "Clark was running late cleaning out the garage. He gets on a project and won't stop until it's perfect. I thought about coming alone but decided to wait for him."

I nodded. "They haven't started yet."

"That's good." She reached over and patted me on the knee. "It's just so good to have you here in church with us. We've been blessed, and our little family is getting bigger, and who knows what the future will bring?" It was not at all a quiet demand for grandchildren.

For the next hour, we prayed for Earl, his family, and for the police to crack the case. I noticed the soft light over the hymn number board was burned out, probably a job Earl would have jumped at doing. At the end of the service, Leslie and Clark left us to go talk to other church members. Up front, several people had stopped to talk to Earl's wife. They exchanged pleasantries and hugs and then moved down the aisle.

"Ben," I said. "Let's go talk to Earl's wife."

"I don't really know her, Dot. Maybe it would be better to send a card."

"And you call yourself a reporter. Don't you realize you have the wife of a murdered man in front of you? People keep telling me how he meddled. Maybe she can give us some insight into all of this."

Ben looked at me, a little surprised. "Yes, I'm a reporter, but don't you think it would be just a tad bit insensitive to interview a woman while she's mourning her dead husband at a prayer service?"

I knew what he was saying was right, and I was way out of line thinking this was a good time to grill the woman on why her husband was such a busybody. She started up the aisle toward us while holding on to her mother-in-law's arm to steady her. When she got closer to us, she stopped.

"It was so nice of you to come," she said to Ben and me. "Earl told me all about your upcoming wedding. I'm sure you have a lot on your mind."

"Thank you so much, and our condolences," Ben said.

"Thank you, although I've heard that so much now, I'm becoming numb. I'm shutting down. My Earl, he was bothered by something before he died, but I was busy with Myrna, his mother. I didn't listen to him. Now I wish I had."

"You couldn't know," I said.

"No. I couldn't. Earl told me you are the young lady who keeps getting into the paper for solving murders. You have a knack for it, he said."

"I was surprised he knew my face from the articles."

"He was a good judge of character. Being the daughter of a minister, that was important to me. Earl was a good man. The best there was. That's why I want you to look into his death. From what he told me, you can figure anything out."

"I don't know about that," I said, feeling the weight of her request hit me.

"I do." She reached over and touched my arm. "I'm counting on you. God bless."

With that, she continued down the aisle, guiding her mother-in-law.

Ben let out a breath. "That was the saddest conversation I've ever had in this church."

I ran a hand under the back of my hair, letting some cool air hit the back of my neck. "I know."

"Let's get out of here. I need some air," Ben said and then made his way to the outer door.

As I left the pew, thinking about relaxing at home after a long day, I heard Vernice talking to Clarence and Charlotte, who were tidying up their music at the altar now that they had turned the overhead lights back on after the prayer service.

"Look what I found." She showed them the paper she had found in the hymnal. "Isn't this strange? What do you think it is?"

"What is what?" Davita came down the aisle after helping her husband shake hands with the exiting parishioners.

"Look." Vernice held it up for all of them to see.

Davita looked and then shook her head. "Beats me." Yawning, she said, "I'm headed home. See you all tomorrow."

Charlotte shrugged, and Clarence went back to putting away music. "It's trash," Clarence said. "Throw it away. You know how people leave things in the pews."

"Who would keep track of their schedule and then forget it in a hymnal holder?" Vernice said. "I hate to say it, but Earl was always good at figuring out things like this. He said he could do the crossword in the paper every morning in ten minutes. Not to speak ill of the dead, but Earl would have been all over this. He was always butting his nose into other people's business. I hate to admit it, but he meddled some in my…affairs. Burned me up. Of course, I kept my Christian behavior in check. The good news is, I guess he took all that stuff he knew about people to the grave." Vernice turned to Ben. "I wish your fiancé, the reporter, would have thought to interview Earl. Then we would know everything about everybody. That's for sure."

"Your boyfriend is a reporter? That must be exciting," Charlotte said.

"Yes," Vernice laughed. "And half the stories he writes are about Dot and her ability to solve crimes the police can't figure out."

"Really?" Charlotte picked up her leather music folio and put it under her arm. "You two are a lot more interesting than I gave you credit for."

"They sure are, and they soon will be husband and wife." Vernice sighed. "I wish Eddie were here. At least he's due back sometime tonight."

"Another trip to Dallas?" Charlotte wiggled her eyebrows upward.

Vernice didn't pick up on Charlotte's slight. "Yes. I don't know what that company would do without him."

Clarence pushed his glasses up on his nose. "Seems awfully convenient if you ask me. Earl dies, and suddenly Eddie has to go out of town. What if that list was his? What if he was tracking him? Maybe he's the one who killed him, and he's gone out of town to bury evidence. I saw that once on Perry Mason. He and Della caught the guy burying things in a forest."

"You're a troubled man, Clarence," Vernice said angrily. "My Eddie would never kill anyone."

"You watch too much TV, Clarence. Seriously, why would anyone want to kill Earl?" Charlotte said. She shooed Clarence away with her hand. "I'm going home. It's been a long day, and Mac is waiting. If I don't get some sort of supper together, he'll starve."

I stifled a yawn as Ben came up and placed his arm around me. "I thought you were right behind me."

Even though Charlotte had quashed Clarence's theory, what he said did make sense. If Eddie really were having an affair and Earl found out about it, Earl could have been pressuring him to end it. I hadn't met Eddie yet, but if he would cheat on his wife, murdering someone is just the next step down.

"I hope you figure out the numbers on that paper, Vernice," Ben said.

"I say there's something funny about it. I should have given it to the pastor to read. I suppose I worry too much," Vernice said.

"I say let's not talk about it anymore. The more we talk about Earl, the less I feel a need to speak ill of the dead," Ben said.

"Good night, you two." As Vernice went down the aisle, Ben leaned down and kissed me on the neck.

"Ben," I whispered. "We're in a church."

"So?"

"We're in a church with your parents standing not ten feet from us."

"We're engaged. They expect this kind of behavior." It did feel good, if not a little taboo. I reached up and placed my hand on his cheek. "I love you too, but now, after kissing me in God's house, your mother is headed this way."

Leslie wagged a finger at us. "You two lovebirds. I should have known better than to leave you alone."

"Caught us," Ben said.

"Would you like to come back to the house for some refreshments? I just baked an apple pie." She wiggled her nose.

"Yum," Ben said.

As much as she wanted me there, I was having an irrational need to have a few more nights as a single woman, not dutiful daughter-in-law Dot. "Uh, I think I'm going to pass. Tomorrow's a busy day. I'm heading home."

Leslie's lips turned into a little pout. "Oh, you're right. You have a lot of responsibilities on you right now. Go get some rest, my dear. The days are ticking down."

Ben nodded. "Maybe next time, Mom."

As we walked out, Ben squeezed my shoulder. "Let me see you to your door, future Mrs. Dalton." Yes, single Dot would love a little visit from single Ben.

Chapter Fourteen

"Thanks for coming with me, Dot," Ellie said as we walked through the park the next evening. The sun was going down, and a slight breeze was kicking up, blowing around some of the ever-present humidity. "Al is out fixing a burnt-out socket at the elementary school before they open up for the kids next week. That building was built before our mothers were born. It's a surprise it still looks as good as it does. Can you believe in just a few years, little Al, Jr. will be going to the same school we did? It's crazy to think about. Anyway, my mom told me that walking before bed will help the baby to settle down and not kick me all night."

I didn't understand how Ellie walking with her legs would tire out the baby's legs, but I had learned at this point in her pregnancy it was best not to argue with her. Even though it was eight in the evening, the sun was still up, but it no longer beat down on us.

"I'm glad to get out of the house. My apartment is pretty well unlivable. I think I moved too many boxes early. Besides that, it doesn't feel the same, you know? It's no longer my home, but the rental house isn't either."

Ellie grabbed my hand and squeezed it gently. "I know. I remember when I packed up to move in with Al. My life was in another place and packed up in boxes."

"Yep. That's the feeling. It also has never been the same since the day you left. I didn't realize how much I would miss you." I loved Ellie's new life with Al and how happy it made her, but I still missed our times together at the end of the day.

"Ahh," Ellie whispered. "I miss you too, especially when Al leaves the lid up on the toilet."

"Ben can't wait for us to be together every day, and I feel the same, most of the time." I should have kept my cold feet to myself, but suddenly I had a need to spill.

Ellie stopped walking and turned directly to me. "That's okay, you know. It's an adjustment learning to live with another person. You're heading into the honeymoon period, and then after that, you'll adjust. It just takes time."

"Okay." I closed my eyes and let the breeze drift over me. When I opened my eyes, I realized there was someone sitting on a park bench not far from us. When I looked closer, I realized it was Earl Gunther's wife. "We should be quiet. That's Earl's wife over there. She might want to be alone."

Ellie peered in the direction of the park bench. "Poor dear. It's so sad she's sitting out here all alone."

"Well, Earl's mother is still alive, so she's not living completely alone."

"Hmm, she's lost her husband, and now it's up to her to take care of his aging parent. This is a lot for one person." It was then that Ellie walked over. "Mrs. Gunther?"

A look of surprise came over the older woman's features. "Yes?" her voice creaked.

"I'm Ellie. I own Bluebonnet's Dress Shop. I just wanted to say I'm so sorry for your loss."

"You are?" Earl's wife still looked wary of Ellie.

"Of course. The whole town has read about it in the paper, and it's a terrible thing. Just terrible."

Earl's wife looked down at a crumpled tissue in her lap. "Thank you. That's very kind of you to say."

Now feeling like an outsider, I joined them and sat down next to Mrs. Gunther. "Is there anything we can do for you?"

She turned and, with a sad smile, shook her head no. "You don't even know me. You don't need to offer to help a stranger." She looked up at Ellie. "When is your baby due?"

Ellie touched her middle. "Very soon. The doctor says the first of September, but Al, Jr. here—that's what I call him, Al, Jr.—is very active."

"May I?" Mrs. Gunther extended a hand toward Ellie.

"Why not? Everyone else does, but they don't ask."

An arthritic hand, curled by age, lay on Ellie's belly. "Oh, I feel him. He's really moving around in there."

"Tell me about it. That's why we're out walking tonight. I'm trying to wear the little tyke out."

She pulled her hand away. "You know, Earl and I always wanted to have children, but it wasn't in God's plan. Some years, it was hard seeing our friends, year after year, add to their families. You are blessed."

"And now, you're going to make me cry," Ellie said.

"No, no. I didn't mean to do that. Where my tears are sad, yours should be joyful."

"How is your husband's mother doing?" I asked.

"Oh, she's sad too. We aren't spending much time together right now. It takes a while to get used to change. Even though we live in the same house, and I take care of her, we each need our time apart. That's why I'm out here tonight. I went for a walk to get out of the house."

"What will you do now?" Ellie asked.

"I don't know. Just go on, I guess. Earl kept me busy, you know? He was always telling me who needed help at church, and I would bake something or go visit. It was kind of like growing up with my father. There's always somebody out there who needs just a little help, a pat on the shoulder, or a prayer. They always say some people marry their fathers, and that's just what I did. He was a good man, but sometimes I wanted to tell him to stay out of things."

"Did he tell you anything about who he was concerned about before he died?"

"That would be both yes and no. He was really concerned about somebody, and I fully expected him to ask me to help. He never did. He said he was bothered by something and had to make a decision about it."

"Bothered about what?"

She shrugged her shoulders upward. "I don't know. He wouldn't tell me, but whatever it was bothered him deeply. He said he needed to do something.

If he did it, it would change a person's life, and if he didn't do it, it would ruin another person's life." She shook her head. "It still doesn't make any sense to me." She rubbed at her temple. "I'm tired. I think I'll walk back home."

"Are you okay by yourself? We'd be glad to walk with you."

She rose from the bench. "No, no. I'm fine." She smiled at Ellie. "Bluebonnet's Dress Shop, huh? I bought my dress for our fortieth anniversary there. After meeting you, I think I'm about to become a regular customer. Good luck with Al, Jr., and enjoy every day of your lives together. They go so fast." She gave a little wave and walked across the park sidewalk to the other side.

"That is so sad. I wish she would have let us walk with her," I said.

"Me too, and you had better bet she's getting a discount when she comes shopping at the store."

"Let's keep going. You need to wear out the baby." We walked through the playground area of the park, now empty of its usual occupants. Summer was almost over, and kids were starting to stockpile pencils and notebooks, getting ready for a new year. Even that made me feel low. I wouldn't be joining them. I was officially an adult now. I knew I was being silly.

I drew closer to Ellie. "So, to change the subject, there were some interesting things going on at the candlelight prayer service for the caretaker at the Camden Chapel."

"Do tell, but first I need to sit down for a minute at that picnic table. This little guy is being very active." She put a hand on her bulging middle and lowered herself down to the wooden bench, reminding me of a limbo move.

"Are you okay?"

"I'm fine. I'm having practice contractions, I'm told. No pain, it just feels like the baby is moving furniture in there. Now tell me what you heard at the service."

I sat down on the bench next to her. "First, and this part is probably not important, but Vernice found some sort of schedule someone had been keeping, hidden in one of the pews. It looked like maybe a time sheet for someone."

"Like work hours? Do they even pay people at a church?"

"It was more than that. It tracked a person all through the day. When they were at work. When they would be home."

"That's weird."

"Yes, well, Vernice was trying to figure it out, but then she said something that concerned me. Did you know she really didn't like Earl?"

"It figures. Now we're getting to the good stuff."

"Now what does that mean?"

"I told you Vernice has gained herself a little bit of a reputation among those of us who work with weddings in this town. She probably didn't like Earl for some stupid reason as well."

I leaned my elbows back on the picnic table as I watched the sun set. "When she makes all those calls, does she get angry? I mean, really angry?"

"Vernice? She's yelled at me, but not every time. I have a feeling she thinks she can kill me with kindness, when she's just killing me."

"Do you think she could really kill someone?"

Ellie wrinkled her brow and scratched the back of her head. "Even if she did, how could she be strong enough to throw Earl over the belfry opening? The paper said he was full of tranquilizers, so he would be dead weight. Right? She doesn't look like she's tuning into the Jack LaLanne exercise program every day. Anyway, if she's making noise about this list she found, why would she do that if she's innocent? I think you're grabbing at theories on her."

Vernice was the same height I was, with about twenty extra pounds. She did have two sons, but lifting Earl wouldn't be the same as lifting a child. "That's a good point. But still, I think I'll talk to Mary about it in the morning. Vernice is not on their list of suspects. It couldn't hurt to let them know she could be extremely pushy if she doesn't get her way."

Ellie started raising herself up belly first. "Sounds good. I'm ready for bed, and I think,"—she crossed her fingers—"so is little Al, Jr."

As we walked out of the park, Ellie quietly rubbing her baby bump as if to settle Al Jr. down, I realized the rhythm of our steps was being matched. Someone was walking behind us, very quietly. Maybe it was just another nighttime park enthusiast, and maybe it wasn't. Either way, I decided not to worry Ellie about it. It would keep her up the rest of the night.

Chapter Fifteen

The next afternoon, I remembered that Vernice had my wedding planner and I needed it back. I had meticulously written down all the different services we were working with, including the phone numbers. I could kick myself for letting her borrow it. My mother's front room was filling up with boxes wrapped in white and silver, wedding gifts sent from friends and relatives far away. We would make a list of the names and addresses for thank you notes, but I wanted it with all the other information, in my notebook, and not floating around. Our plan had been to preaddress the thank-you cards so we could get them in the mail quickly after the wedding.

Aunt Mavis was over, helping my mother put up some of the last of the summer tomatoes. The house was steamy, and the scent of tomato sauce was in the air. This was a yearly ritual that would have us in tomato sauce until January at least.

"If you're worried about losing names and addresses, you should call Vernice and get your book back," Mom said while she peeled the skin off of a tomato. "I think she's had it long enough."

I would have called Vernice's house, but the only place I had her phone number recorded was in the book. I would have to stop over instead. "Every time I get anywhere near Vernice it takes her forever to stop talking. I could probably just pick it up tomorrow." I could feel the heat of the kitchen sinking into my skin. Sweat was running down my temples.

"Nonsense," Aunt Mavis said abruptly. "Let me go with you. I can shut up a chatterbox. I have no use for women who have to constantly hear the sound of their own voice."

Normally, I would decline my aunt's offer. She had a way of commandeering a room, and that could lead to problems, but today I was thankful for her talent.

"Would you really?"

"Anything for you, Buttercup." Aunt Mavis could be gruff when she ordered us around like an army unit about to go into battle, but deep inside, she was a cupcake with a gooey filling.

A few minutes later, I was still thankful, but mostly because we had escaped from my mother's hot kitchen. Even with a supermarket full of canned goods, she insisted on canning. It was probably because she grew up in the Depression and planned ahead for days when the paycheck didn't last out the bills, but it never happened. The canning process was hot and exhausting. I also didn't have much appreciation for my father's favorite, pickled eggs. Why do that to a perfectly good egg?

When we drove up to Vernice's house, the lawn was beautifully manicured. There were yellow marigolds planted all the way up the sidewalk, and on each side of the doorway, there were large pots of what looked like oregano. I put the car in Park. "She keeps talking about getting ready for her boys to come home from camp. I'm not sure if they've come back yet. They've been in Fredericksburg since June. I didn't know summer camps lasted that many weeks. I guess with her husband working so much, it was just easier to let them spend the summer elsewhere. From the looks of her house, she's been working hard to make it look perfect for them."

"Good. She'll be too busy to talk," Mavis got out of the car and strode up the walk.

Following her like a dutiful niece, I hoped she was right. I rang the doorbell and waited for the sound of Vernice's footsteps coming our way on the other side. The house was very quiet. No music. No dog barking. No kids yelling. I rang the doorbell again, thinking maybe she had water running or was in the back yard.

"Maybe she's not home," Mavis said. "I say we abort this mission. You'll have to get it later when she's home."

I turned and looked at the driveway. "That's her car. She has to be home." I rang the doorbell a third time. If she didn't hear this, then I'd have to come back.

"Maybe," Mavis said, a disapproving look on her face, "she's over at the neighbor's talking their ear off."

"She told me she doesn't get along with her neighbors. Something about a property line dispute."

"Sounds like Vernice," Mavis said. "Can't say I'm surprised."

I gave up on the doorbell and decided to knock on the door. When I did, the door pushed open slightly. It was unlocked and not even closed. I stepped inside Vernice's house.

"Vernice? Are you here?" No answer. "It's Dot Morgan, Vernice. I needed to get my wedding planning notebook from you."

Aunt Mavis came in behind me, and with the moves of Robert Stack in *The Fugitive,* she began rapidly stepping from room to room. For a minute there, I was glancing at her hands to see if she was holding a gun like the cops do in the movies.

"Vernice?" I repeated, my voice dying in the still air of the three-bedroom ranch home.

I stepped across the living room, heading for the kitchen, when Aunt Mavis stopped me in the doorway. Her face had taken on a pale green tint.

"Need you to find the phone. We need to call the police."

"Is she hurt?" I tried to look around my aunt's body block.

"I think it's more than that."

I wiggled forward and looked over Aunt Mavis's shoulder. Vernice was on the floor in the fetal position. She had dried vomit coming out of her mouth. Next to her was a bottle of pills and a note.

"Has she…"

Mavis put a steadying hand on my arm. "I don't know, Dot, but if she has even a little bit of a chance of surviving, we need the medics here. I'm going to try and find a pulse."

I turned around and, after a quick search, found the phone in the living room. After reporting what I had witnessed, I hung up and returned to where Aunt Mavis now stood guard next to Vernice. There were dark brown crumbs mixed with white icing and flecks of carrot on her pale blue face. It looked like she had eaten carrot cake before dying.

"Is that cake on her lips? Do you think it was food poisoning? Is there a carrot cake anywhere? Something baked?"

Aunt Mavis looked around. "Don't see anything."

I hated doing it, but I looked back at the dried throw-up around Vernice's mouth. It didn't make any sense. Did she eat cake and then overdose?

"This is going to sound pretty unfeeling," Mavis suggested in a whisper, "but if you see your notebook, I suggest grabbing it before the police take it. You've spent a lot of time putting all that information together."

"What if there is a clue on it or in it?"

Mavis shrugged. "I doubt it, but if you find something, say something."

I looked and found the notebook on a small desk in her bedroom. A piece of paper lay next to it with a handwritten list of the sections I had created for the wedding. I quickly paged through the notebook, but nothing was any different. I clutched it under my arm as the police started pounding on the door.

Once again, I was smack dab in the middle of what looked to be a murder. Not the wedding gift I was wanting, and Camden Chapel had another member down.

Chapter Sixteen

"Yes, Aunt Mavis and I discovered her right there in her kitchen. Thank goodness her kids are still at camp," I said to Ben while holding one finger in my other ear, trying to drown out Aunt Mavis as she recounted the story to my parents behind me in the kitchen.

Ben asked, "Are you sure she was dead?"

"Her coloring was funny, especially around her mouth." I wasn't sure how to describe the next part. Maybe I was focusing on the wrong thing, but I couldn't get it out of my mind. "She had been eating something when she died. Carrot cake? And there was…I don't know."

"What?" he asked. "Think about it, Dot. You are the first on the scene. The paper will want details."

Mavis was launching into her description simultaneously, her voice rising as she neared the description of the body. She was so loud I could barely hear Ben, so I tried to stretch the phone cord farther, but felt the phone almost skid across the table where it rested.

"Just tell me. What did you see? Think of yourself as a reporter. Who, what, when, where, why. Give me some descriptive details."

I tried to think of myself as a reporter with a camera, taking pictures of poor Vernice's dead body. "There were crumbs on her lips and on the floor."

"Okay," Ben said in what I now knew was his patient voice. He'd be a great father someday. "So she had a piece of cake."

"There was no cake."

"No cake? I thought you just said there were cake crumbs on her lips."

"No cake. There were crumbs around Vernice's mouth like she had eaten something, but there was no cake on the counter. I looked for it. That meant if it was food poisoning, it would still be there, but if someone poisoned that cake, it could be they took it away because it's the murder weapon."

Ben was silent on the other end of the line, then he said, "You know, Dot. Losing Vernice is strange, and I'm very sorry you had to be the one to discover her. The police can't be sure of anything yet; the investigation is so new. That being said, this puts you in the middle of two murder cases."

"I was afraid you would say that. Thank goodness my notebook wasn't lost. I don't know what I'd do if I had to start all over again."

"What notebook?"

"You know. The notebook I'm using to keep track of all the wedding details."

"Oh, that notebook. What does that have to do with Vernice?"

"I loaned it to her. She wanted to make a copy for future brides and their weddings. I was over there to get it back. The gifts are piling up, and I needed to keep track of addresses for the thank-you notes."

"So where is the notebook now?" he asked.

"Oh, I have it. I grabbed it before the police got there."

"You did what? How do you know there weren't clues on the notebook? Fingerprints? Stuff like that?"

"I doubt it. The notebook was in another room away from Vernice's body," I said, hoping he understood how important it was to me.

"You are also in the middle of having a wedding on Saturday. I know I can't stop you from trying to find out more, but I would ask that you don't forget the wedding day. Deal?"

I felt acid rising up in my chest. The idea of missing my own wedding because I was the main suspect in two murders danced around in the back of my mind. "Ben! Of course, I'm onboard with the wedding thing."

"The wedding thing? That's how you look at it? I can't believe out of the two of us, I'm the more romantic one."

His statement shocked me. I grew up on Doris Day movies. How could he say I wasn't romantic? I felt like I needed to remind him I was the girl. I'd never met a man who was so sentimental.

"You know what I mean," I said. "And you also know I love you very much and am pretty desperate to marry you."

"Thank you for that, and I love you, too. The police will find out who killed Vernice, and they'll figure out your clue about cake crumbs and no cake. Trust me."

"I trust you, and I would ask you to trust me, Ben Dalton."

"Uh huh." He didn't sound convinced. I needed to work on my persuasion skills.

Ben hung up just as Mavis finished her story, which, with a few exaggerations, now placed her on the scene trying to give life-saving support while I cowered in a corner.

My mom reached out for my hand. "Poor Dot. It must have been awful for you."

"I'm fine, Mom. Thanks. I'm just really glad Aunt Mavis was there with me."

"Are you sure you're fine?" Now my father was giving me his worried face.

"Please don't worry. Like I said, I'm fine. Sadly, Vernice is not the first dead body I've come across." I picked up my notebook. "If you don't mind, I'm going to step into the next room and write down the addresses from the gifts. Ben made sure to tell me that he wanted me to keep my focus on the wedding. I'm going to review what Vernice and I were doing and plan from there."

My father beamed. "That's my girl."

I stepped into the front room and opened the wedding book. Going to the note section at the back I began a list.

Earl is pushed off the belfry.

Vernice is probably poisoned.

Then a question.

Who would have the most to gain from killing these two people?

Wedding planning? Not right now.

Chapter Seventeen

"I can't believe you and my mom stumbled on her," Ellie said as we took a coffee break from packing boxes in my apartment. Arlene brought us up coffee on a tray along with some of her oatmeal raisin cookies.

"Your mom found her first. It's awful to think about Vernice's poor children coming home from camp to find their mother murdered. Her husband wasn't around as usual, so it was just her in the middle of the kitchen. Vernice could be pushy, but she didn't deserve a death like that.

"Yeah, well, thank goodness the boys were at camp. They would never forget the picture in their heads if they had found her."

"Yes. Mary told me it took the police a while to find Eddie."

"Which motel did they find him at?" Ellie sneered.

"Don't say that. Anyway, the camp counselors had to wait for him to drive over to Fredericksburg to pick up the boys."

"That could not have been easy. She spent all the time and effort in raising those boys. Now he has to tell them that their mother is dead? The woman who arranged everything for them. How is he going to handle all the day-to-day stuff like school and meals when he's out of town all the time?"

Ellie, who had always been our "family career girl," sounded suddenly maternal. More and more, she was focusing on children around her. She was already fiercely protective of her unborn son. Lord help whoever crossed her when anyone threatened him.

"I guess Eddie got the boys back safe and sound," I said.

"Vernice always talked about how wonderful he was, but I never met him. It was strange they had trouble finding him because she did say he was home more often now."

"Do you think he did it?" I asked.

"Did what?"

"You know. Do you think he murdered Vernice so that he could marry his mistress?" I had only heard about marriages that came to such severe measures, but if I had been married to Vernice, who knew what I might have been capable of.

"Be serious. That's a little much, even for a guy who cheats on his wife. I will tell you one thing I heard about him, though. Barbara told me that someone was in the store this morning who told her Joe at Proper Printing heard from the waitresses at Columbo's that the pastor's wife was going to help him with some of the kid duties."

"You mean Davita Ross?"

"Yes, her. Isn't that interesting?"

"Yes." I had put that theory to rest. After hearing what the town gossip train had to say, I revisited the thought of Davita being the other woman. Maybe that packed suitcase had more to do with Eddie than her chance at stardom. It worked to give a motive, but I distinctly remembered her saying she didn't want kids. Being with Eddie would mean instant child-rearing responsibility. Was she so in love with him she was willing to give up her dream? I grabbed my wedding planner and made a few notes on the hidden case pages about Davita while Ellie talked.

Finally, Ellie yawned. "I'm about ready for my nap. I think I ate more cookies than I packed boxes."

"You were a great help," I said as she left a minute later. Not only with the packing, but with giving me a new direction on Davita. Some killers are right out in the open where you least expect them. A pastor's wife would be a prime suspect in an Agatha Christie mystery. As soon as I finished writing down my thoughts, the phone rang.

"Thank goodness. I was worried you had already shut off the phone." It was my mother and her daily call about the wedding. I would be so glad when it was all over. I stopped myself. This was the most memorable day of my life. I just needed to live through getting to it.

"Hi, Mom."

"I know you're busy these days, but I wanted to remind you of the wedding shower tomorrow at the library. We're setting up in the community room, and I made all the staff promise to give you something besides a book."

I had known this was coming up, but circumstances kept pushing it to the back of my mind. Usually with something like this, my mother and I would work together to make it happen, planning out everything from refreshments to the guest list. Lately, I'd forgotten it, my head so filled with wedding preparations.

"I haven't forgotten," I fibbed, although it was close to being at the end of my priority list.

"That's a relief. I know getting ready to throw a wedding is all-consuming. Is there anything else you need me to do to help? I really appreciated Vernice taking over, but in a way, it feels like she usurped my job. Now that she's gone, I'm worried we've missed something."

She was right. Vernice had pulled together every little detail. All I did was report back to my mom, and every time, no matter who we were dealing with, there weren't any problems. What would this time have been like without helpful Vernice? I hadn't thought of having a wedding coordinator, but Leslie was so dead set on it, and Ben wanted to please his mother so badly, I never even considered saying no. What I heard in my mother's voice told me that my quick decision had hurt her. I was the only daughter she had, and she was attending my wedding as more of a guest than the mother of the bride. I tried to think of something she could help with and came up empty.

"Uh, I'm so happy you're giving the bridal shower. Thank you so much for putting it together."

"Oh, that's nothing, a labor of love. Besides, all the ladies feel like you're one of their children. Alvira from Reference has pretty well documented every picture, every visit, every event they witnessed when you were growing up. She has a better scrapbook than your father, and I do."

"She has?"

"Oh yes. The ladies have been brewing for weeks over what the perfect gift would be for their little Dot." The library ladies. In a way, they were just like Leslie Dalton's Camden church ladies. A community of women who held each other up in good times and bad. It did feel sort of like they were the fairies and I was Cinderella. Bippity Boppity…your book is due. We love you.

"I'm also glad Mavis told you to get your book back. You're going to have to write more thank-you notes, you know. More gifts, more thank yous."

It was hard for me to understand why the same people who were giving me wedding gifts had to also give me a shower gift.

"That is so sweet, Mom. I love your library ladies, and I promise I'll be there with my 'thank you for the toaster' smile."

"Very good, because from what I hear, you may be using it several times." She paused for a moment, and I wondered if she was still on the line. "Your father and I are so excited you've found your one true love. I think you're going to have a wonderful marriage and a wonderful life."

A wonderful life. Why was it that at weddings everyone talked about forever, but in real life, it didn't always work out that way? My mind was already racing back to Davita and a possible connection to Eddie as I hung up the phone. Maybe they had been using the local hotel to meet? Could I track their receipts? That would give one or both motives to kill Vernice, but what about Earl? Could it be possible there were two unconnected murders in the same town within days of each other? It was possible, but not probable. Plus, really, a pastor's wife knocking off the church wedding lady? I was still in this train of thought when I received my next phone call of the morning.

"Dot, it's Leslie. How are you doing, sweetheart?" Her voice rose in excitement. "We heard the news of how you found our dear Vernice. How terrible for you." This was really nice of her to call. It made me feel better about disappointing her with my plans to work after I married.

"Yes. It was pretty awful."

"And exactly not the kind of thing a girl should be exposed to right before her wedding. This should be a time of wonderment, not murder. It's just too bad our Benjamin wasn't there to shield you."

"I'm fine. My Aunt Mavis was with me, and she served in the army. There isn't much she's afraid of, even finding a body."

She continued, "Everyone at Camden Chapel feels so awful that these horrible things have happened right before the blessed nuptials, we have arranged a little surprise for you."

I couldn't imagine what the surprise could be and was almost afraid to ask. "Surprise?"

"Yes, ma'am. It's all very last-minute, but we've pulled it off. We ladies have put together a wedding shower. Very unorganized, mind you, but we're even putting up some crepe paper in the fellowship hall. Are you excited?"

"Uh, yes, of course. That's so nice, but—" How would she react when she found out her grand gesture had already been upstaged by my mother?

"It was really quite exciting, how it came together so quickly, but that's what a bunch of women do when they put their minds to it."

"Wonderful, but—"

"So, we need you at the fellowship hall tomorrow at 1:30." Then she finished off her announcement with another, "Surprise!"

Her voice was so filled with hope of my response to the gesture. I wasn't sure what to say.

"We still have some ladies to pull in." She was almost out of breath. "But I think you'll be tickled pink with all the gifts the ladies are bringing for your new home with my son."

She hung up so quickly, I was left with only one thought. The two showers were thirty minutes apart. How could I be in two places at the same time? If I called her back to tell her I already had a shower to go to, it would hurt her feelings as well as damage the beginnings of the future bond we would share, but what about my mother and the ladies at the library? How could I please everyone at the same time?

That's when it struck me, I wasn't in this all by myself. I would call Ben. He would know the best way to handle his mother, and if he didn't, I might have even bigger problems.

Chapter Eighteen

When I dialed Ben, he answered the phone with a hurried hello.

"Hello, Mrs. Dalton."

"Not yet, but I like the sound of it. Do you have a minute?"

"I have just a minute. With two possible murders to cover, we are hopping with assignments. The boss wants us to interview anyone who might even be remotely connected to the victims. Even your name is on the list."

"Great, but that's not why I'm calling. I have a little problem on the wedding front. Your mother has pulled together a quick wedding shower for me tomorrow at 1:30."

He didn't answer right away, and I could tell he was probably either reading or writing something. Finally, he spoke. "I think that sounds like a good thing, right?"

"Yes. It's very thoughtful, and from the sound of it, a lot of work on her part. The problem is my mother and Aunt Mavis are giving a shower at practically the same time."

"Oh, that's not good. Did you tell her that?"

"I tried. I don't know what to do."

There were muffled sounds at the other end of the phone conversation, making me think Ben had put the receiver end of the phone against his chest. Finally, he came back on the line. "Listen, Dot. You need to call my mom back and talk to her. I'm sure she'll understand. Have to go. They want me to interview Earl's fishing buddy. Him and half the town."

I hung up the phone, not feeling any better about the double shower situation. The stack of sheet music Davita had given me to look through was still piled on my coffee table. I absentmindedly leafed through them, wondering just how Ben could solve my problem when he was so busy with his job. I was late in picking a song, but without Vernice nagging me, the music choice had been pushed from my thoughts.

I was down to "Unchained Melody" by The Righteous Brothers, "Can't Help Falling in Love" by Elvis, or "At Last" by Etta James. I was so happy the church was allowing us to have one popular piece of music along with the traditional hymns. Many churches looked down on current music, but for our wedding, I wanted something that reflected us, not some musician who wrote a song before the turn of the century. It was going to make the day even more special.

Hating the fact Ben was so busy he couldn't hold a phone conversation, I needed to get my mind off the timing of the showers. I decided to see if I could get more information out of Davita, like, for instance, if she was having an affair with the one and only Eddie. What would I do if I not only found out she and Eddie were involved in a torrid affair, but together they plotted to kill Vernice? It couldn't be right. If Eddie was even a little bit of the man Vernice claimed he was, he wouldn't murder his wife. Then there was Davita, a pastor's wife, who, although she felt boxed in, still was a nice person. I could see a door-to-door salesman killing Vernice because she wouldn't shut up, but not the wife of a pastor.

Davita was unhappy with her role in life, but I didn't see any killer instinct in her, unless it was for the chance to sing at a supper club.

As I stepped out of my apartment, Ellie was waddling up the sidewalk, her hand on her back, her face flushed from the heat. She wore a white and pink dotted maternity dress with tiny straps exposing her pink shoulders, roasting in the sun. She had made several dresses for her changing body, and all of them were inspired. I encouraged her to add a maternity line to her store along with the bridal dresses. I was sure there were a few brides who might be shopping for both bridal and maternity wear, and if they shared a secret upcoming event, Ellie would keep any unplanned pregnancies quiet. She might have quite a booming yet confidential business on the side.

Ellie's cheeks were too pink. "Are you okay?" I asked. "Are you having the baby?"

"No." She placed a hand on her protruding belly. It looked like it had multiplied fivefold in size since I had seen her last. Could the baby actually grow that fast? What would she look like by the wedding? She had proudly shown me all the extra panels of material she had artfully installed in the empire waist of her maid of honor dress, but my new cousin's bulk might have outdone her efforts.

She looked down at the baby-to-be. "At least I don't think so. I wanted to ask you a crime-solving-type question."

"Shouldn't you ask Mary something like that?"

"Maybe, but you are easier to get to, and these days the easy way is the best way."

"What can I do? Do you know something new about Earl or Vernice?"

"Sorry, no." She hesitated. "Promise me you won't say I'm being silly, but how does a person really know when they're being followed?"

"You think someone is following you? Since when?"

Ellie gestured, "Can we talk about it in the shade?" We moved under the giant red oak tree in the front yard to get out of the sun.

"Since a few days ago. It's a man, but every time I try to get a look at him, he gets away. What little I've seen of him doesn't help. I've lived in this town my whole life, but I've never seen this guy before."

"Did you tell Al?"

"Sure did. He's been trying to catch the guy, but no luck. Maybe I'm just being silly and all. Pregnant crazy brain."

"Maybe you're not. Look what has been going on with the members of the Camden Chapel. Maybe Earl and Vernice had a guy following them, too. We just don't know at this point."

"But I don't belong to that church. Do you think this little creep following me might have something to do with the caretaker's murder? Why? What did I ever do? Man, one ladies' lunch and I'm on the hit list."

"Who would follow around a pregnant woman? You're not looking anything like the girls on the calendar in the Camden Car Repair garage."

"Yeah, well, neither did Earl. I don't know, but for right now, I want you to stick with me. Can you do that? Maybe I can get a look at the guy."

"I was hoping you would say that. Let's go talk to Davita Ross. I finally picked out my song for the wedding."

"You hadn't picked your song yet? This close to the wedding? What were you going to do? Hand her the sheet music when you walk down the aisle?"

I hung my head down. "I know. I should have told her weeks ago, but I wanted to feel like I had picked the perfect song."

Ellie laughed and squeezed my side. "Oh, Dot. Whether or not the song is perfect doesn't matter. You're marrying the perfect guy."

"I am?" I wasn't sure why I said that so quickly. I couldn't wait to marry Ben, and yet I felt this weird sense of uncertainty.

"That's what he told me." She winked.

"Of course he did. I know I'm being silly, but as Ben's mom likes to tell me, this is the only wedding I'll ever have."

We started walking to my car, the sun waiting to pounce as soon as we were out from under the tree's canopy of shuttering leaves.

"Gee," Ellie said. "I wonder if Liz Taylor's mother ever said that to her." I stopped walking to laugh. Thank God for Ellie and her sense of humor.

"If she did, she forgot about it somewhere between husbands." I giggled.

We found Davita Ross planting flowers outside the parsonage. She looked up from her kneeling position next to the flower bed and pushed back the straw-colored floppy hat that was protecting her from the heat of the sun.

"Hello there. What brings you out in this heat?" She swiped a gloved hand across her forehead, glistening with sweat. The kohl eyeliner she used to achieve an upturned cat eye was slightly smeared on one side.

"I wanted to give you my sheet music for your solo. Sorry it took so long."

Davita pulled herself up using only the strength of her legs. "That's fine. You're not the first bride to turn music in right before the wedding." She looked at the sheet music. "'At Last.' That's a good one, and I love getting the chance to sing it. I like it."

Ellie moved forward, trying to gently approach, but she carried it off like a rhino pulling itself up a hill. "I heard you were helping Vernice's husband get his kids settled. Do they know who killed Vernice?"

I was pretty sure it was the rule of pastors' wives not to gossip about the flock, but as Davita started removing her gardening gloves, finger by finger, I could tell she had something on her mind.

"The police haven't shared anything with me, but it's become pretty clear that Eddie certainly doesn't measure up to all the bragging Vernice did about him. I helped hire Mrs. Morrison from Baylor Street to watch the boys now that they're back. Vernice must have done everything for those boys. He didn't know where their socks were or what kinds of food they liked, and he didn't even know what grade his oldest was in. He seemed out of it, which you can't begrudge him. His wife just died, and I don't like to say things like this." She paused as if considering if she should share this next bit of news, "But I smelled alcohol on his breath."

News of Eddie's distracted parenting was not what I expected from Davita. If she were having romantic liaisons with the man, she should at least seem to like him.

"Did he ever say where he was when she died?" I asked.

"You mean like an alibi? He told me he was making a sales call in some new territory his company had assigned him to. He said they went out for drinks, and he had a few too many, so he chose not to drive home. He got a motel out on the highway." She fanned herself with her hat. "Sounds sketchy to me."

Ellie leaned closer, trying to lessen the distance between her height and petite Davita. "Sure, it does," she said conspiratorially. "You know how they say the wife is always the last to know."

"It's amazing he was out with a client on a weeknight. What a life this guy has. Roger and I spent the night watching *The Red Skelton Hour* and then went to bed." She looked out wistfully. "Sometimes I wish I was the man."

"Can I ask you something?" I asked.

"Sure," Davita answered.

"Did you ever think," I winked, "Eddie was handsome?"

She snorted slightly when she laughed. "Him? I guess if you like that kind of guy. He had some nice features, but he wasn't really my type."

"Oh," Ellie nodded. "You mean you prefer men who look like Pastor Ross."

"Uh, I didn't say that either, now did I? Dealing with one man is quite enough for me." She hugged the sheet music to her chest. "I'll get to practicing the music. Good choice. I guess I'll see you tomorrow at the shower."

"Uh, about that. I think I might be a little late."

She clucked her tongue. "Ooh. Not good for the newest bride of Camden Chapel."

I considered whether I should make an excuse or tell the truth. "To be honest with you, my mother had already planned a shower for me at the library a half an hour before the Camden Chapel ladies. I'm trying to make it to both."

Davita's eyes widened. "And neither knows?"

"No."

"Oh my. You poor thing. Hope you can pull it off. I've broken rules with the ladies a few times, and it's never easy."

As Davita let herself into the house, Ellie nudged me. "I know exactly what you were doing. You weren't giving her music, you were giving her the third degree."

I put my arm through hers. "You got me. Only I was sure she was having an affair with Eddie. Now, I don't think so."

"Somehow," Ellie said, "I think she's smarter than that." She put a hand to her back. "Listen, I'm loving all this sleuthing you're doing, but I feel like heading home and putting my feet up. I'm getting a killer backache. I'm not seeing that guy anywhere, so maybe you scared him off."

I needed to meet Ben at the rental house, but would have just enough time to drop Ellie back at her car. "No problem. Are you okay?"

"Sure, sure. I'm fine."

After making sure Ellie was safely behind the wheel of her car, I rushed to our rental house to meet Ben. We had an appointment with Al, who agreed to look at a couple of bedroom lights that weren't working. The home had been built in the 1920s and was a small two-story with a wide front porch. My favorite thing about it when we first saw it was the oak tree in the front yard and the swing on the porch. I could see us living there, swinging on a warm summer evening, listening to the wind blowing through the trees.

It represented peace for the two of us. The red brick on the home was weathered from decades of rain and a couple of hurricanes, but the windows, although somewhat sticky, were still in good shape with the original wood frames.

We had a detached garage with a narrow driveway, which would only fit one car. There was a back door off the kitchen with a concrete set of stairs that led to the driveway. Inside, the wallpaper stood proudly above the chair rails, and all the light fixtures were original. There was a large picture window that looked out onto the front porch with a great view of the street, which was just a few blocks off the main street. I would be able to walk to town anytime I needed to.

"You got here first," Ben said as he exited his car.

"I'm surprised. I thought I was late."

"Al's not here?" he asked.

"Nope. Let's go in. It's hot out here."

I took my key out of my purse and stepped onto the front porch. Even though the house looked cozy and serene on the outside, the inside was in a state of chaos. The house was stuffy but cooler than outside. A lone easy chair that Ben had brought over using Al's truck, sat against one wall, as well as a second-hand couch from Ben's parents. We had a table phone next to it on the floor, hooked up by Southwestern Bell a few weeks ago, after we waited half a day for the installer to show up. We had a carpet for the wood floors, but it was still rolled up and resting against a wall, and taped-up boxes sat everywhere, waiting for the endless job of opening and putting away items.

In the bedroom was a new queen-sized mattress and box spring still covered in plastic leaning up against the wall, as well as pieces of a bed frame. Neither Ben nor I had a double bed, so all these pieces were new.

"Maybe we should use this time and put the bed together," Ben said with an unmistakable leer in his eye.

"The bed is the first thing they say you should put together when you move," I winked back.

We went about assembling the frame, tightening the bolts, and putting in the slats. From there, we added the box spring and finally the mattress. Once it thumped into place, fitting snugly in the frame, we fell backwards onto the bed and then into each other's arms.

"I think I like this room the best," Ben said, planting kisses on my neck. This was one of the few times we had together in complete privacy and with enough room. We weren't on a couch, a single bed, or—God forbid—sitting in a car with a stick shift between us.

As Ben continued to kiss me, blazing a trail of heat through my body, I began to think about where we were headed, and as enjoyable a thought as that was, I sat straight up. "Stop. Al's going to walk in on us."

Ben was not stopping. "We're engaged. He'll understand," he murmured.

"Ben."

He was beginning to unbutton my blouse.

"Ben! How would you feel if you walked in and saw Ellie and Al like this?"

That stopped him cold. His one-word answer said it all. "Eww." He wrinkled his nose in disgust.

I sat up and re-buttoned my blouse. "He's really late. Maybe we should call him."

Ben sat up and ran a hand through his hair. "Good idea. He might be at the shop and has forgotten the time."

"I say we call their house first. Maybe it has something to do with Ellie and the baby."

When we called Ellie and Al's home, Al answered on the second ring.

"Al, we're waiting for you," Ben said.

"Dad gummit. I'm sorry. Ellie called me at the shop and said she's having labor pains. I thought we were going to the hospital. Her mama came over, and it turns out she's having something called Braxton Hicks. Her body is pushing her around, but she's not having the baby yet. I'm sorry. Meeting you just flew right out of my mind."

"So, she's not having the baby?" I asked.

Ben put his hand over the receiver of the phone. "No. She's having some sort of pushing thing going on, though, but she's not in labor. Al was so worried about her, he forgot about us."

Ben got back on the phone. "Don't worry about us. We can do this another day. Take care of Ellie."

"Thanks, brother. It feels like I'm walking a tightrope right now with all the baby doings."

After Ben hung up, I picked up my bag. "I should probably go over there and check on Ellie." I looked around the house. "Soon, it'll all be ours, and we'll be living here. I can't wait."

Ben pulled me close. "Me either."

Chapter Nineteen

The library community room was decorated with white balloons and silver ribbons. This was a multipurpose room often used for elections and local author book sales. The library staff also held all their staff parties here and today it was set up cafeteria-style, with tables divided into two sections. On one side I recognized my mother's punch bowl and a stack of little sandwiches with the crusts cut off. Very Julia Child. On the other side was a heaping pile of gifts wrapped in white and silver paper. How many gifts did one new marriage need?

"Welcome, bride-to-be." Aunt Mavis's gravelly voice sounded from behind me. "Right on time." A large white corsage, featuring a beautiful silver bow, was attached to my dress. Beneath the flowers was a small plastic pin discreetly displaying the word "Bride."

I had remembered to bring my notebook so I could record the names for thank yous. I set it on the end of the table.

"Hello, baby," my mother said. "How are you doing so close to the big day?" She pulled me into a hug. I had always thought of myself as a strong and independent woman but finding myself in the embrace of my mom nourished a silent need. She would always be there to love and protect me. Whether it was a scraped knee or a broken heart, she had been there, and she would be in the future.

She pulled back and straightened a stray lock of hair that had fallen on my forehead. "Well, you look beautiful as usual."

Ellie had made me a few outfits for the summer that were in style for 1965. Some people shopped at Sears or JCPenney, but I had Ellie. My favorite dress she had made for me was a simple black shift with white laces crisscrossing the front bodice. It was so sophisticated, and I felt like Liz Taylor when I wore it, even if I more closely resembled Sandra Dee. Today I wore a white, red, and black color-blocked dress that she made after seeing an ad for Yves St. Laurent. It was a simple sleeveless shift, but the contrast of the colors was beautiful.

"Thank you. Listen, I need to tell you about something. Ben's mom—" Before I could let her know, a voice behind me interrupted us.

"Congratulations, Chica!" Mary, still in uniform, came over holding a large gift. "Never thought you'd ever make an honest man out of him."

Mary put down the gift and gave me a rocking hug, very unbecoming of a police officer. "Don't look too closely at the wrapping job. The kids wanted to help wrap their beloved Tia Dot's gift. I think they like you more than their real tias."

"I'm so glad you made it." Even though the library ladies were like family to me, Mary felt like a sister. From the day we met, and she offered me half her sandwich, I knew I liked her.

"Yeah, well, Officer Jerry was against my leaving my post, but our new lead detective, Fabio Barrerra, told me to go. He said something about it being a good idea to have an officer on the scene if you were going to find any more bodies." She looked around. "Where is Ellie?"

Mavis stepped up. "That girl has been running late to everything. This time it's something about Al. I never know these days."

I wondered if she had mentioned to Mavis the feeling of being followed. But then again, Ellie had probably kept it to herself. Aunt Mavis could be overwhelming if she thought she had a mission to complete, especially when it came to her daughter.

"What about Al?" Mary asked, curious.

"I'm not sure. Until that baby comes, I try not to ask too many questions. Do you know she sent her poor husband out for sardines and graham crackers the other night? I think she's suffering from baby battle fatigue." Mavis looked around. "Let's get on with the festivities for little Dot."

I checked my watch. It was 1:07. I had only twenty-three minutes left before I would need to rush off to the next shower. If I started opening gifts right now, I might be finished in time to skip out. I mentally started calculating how much time it would take me to travel from the library to Camden Chapel. At this point, I would be a little late, but there was a possibility that I could get away with it. I had to start things on this end.

"Let's open gifts," I said, clapping my hand a little too loudly, making some of the more skittish librarians jump and push up their glasses.

"Oh," my mother's eyes looked surprised, then she said, "We can."

"Good. Let's get moving." I marched over to the gift table while my mother scurried around behind me, grabbing a pad of paper and a pen.

I pulled at the card. "Let's see who this is from." I rolled off a name like a bingo caller on a Sunday night. My mother scribbled it in my notebook, creating the list that would be referred to when I wrote the legions of thank-you notes waiting for me.

We were given three chafing dishes, two toasters, and five Tupperware sets. I would be burping those little lids way into the future. I had three gifts left when I glanced at my watch. It was 1:30 already. I pictured my mother-in-law's face as she watched the door, waiting for her future family member. It would be humiliating for her. My frustration was leading me close to tears. Why did this wedding business mean I spent most of my time making other people happy? Isn't it their job to do that for me?

A sinking feeling hit me as I grabbed the next gift. I was foolish to think I could magically pull this off. My finger strayed at the curlicue ribbon when I heard footsteps at the door.

"Hello, ladies," Davita Ross stood in front of the women from Camden Chapel, who were carrying gifts, food, and what looked like a replica of my mother's punch bowl in Leslie Dalton's arms. She carefully moved forward and set it on the table next to the nearly empty library version. Library ladies could get very thirsty. Davita continued. "We heard our Dot here had not one but two showers going on and was too nice to hurt anyone's feelings, so we decided to crash yours."

Leslie then came close and whispered in my ear. "You should have told me, sweetheart. I would have understood. Davita shared it with us."

"Sorry," I apologized. I felt a huge sense of relief and fought the tears welling in my eyes.

She squeezed my forearm gently. "Don't be. I won't bite."

Charlotte came up behind us. "I wouldn't be too sure of that."

"You made it!" Aunt Mavis's voice echoed over the rising sound level in the room.

Ellie, her face flushed, made her way across the crowded room. "I'm sorry I'm late. I was waiting for Al to call me, and I fell asleep on the couch."

"Al's a grown man. You don't need to worry so much about him," Aunt Mavis said.

"Get all the rest you can," Charlotte said. "Once that baby comes, you won't have a minute to yourself. My sister has three kids, and I don't think she's sat down since 1961."

Other ladies around us laughed knowingly. Ellie, meanwhile, had that deer-in-the-headlights look.

"What happened with Al?" Mavis asked.

Ellie shook her head. "Al is a born talker. He got into a conversation with one of his buddies from the VFW and lost track of time. I'm a little nervous, with the baby so close to coming."

Minnie Gardner, one of the weekend librarians, came over, pulling her cardigan closer. "Dot, your fiancé is on the phone for you."

"He is?"

"Yes, you can take it in the back office."

I was feeling pretty good at how things had turned out when I punched the blinking button on the phone. I worried he would tell me they had found somebody else dead. "Hey," he said. "Sorry to pull you away from the shower. Did we get any good stuff?"

"Yes. I hope you like Tupperware. What's the matter?"

"A strange thing happened, and I thought you would like to know about it. I got a letter from Vernice."

"Vernice? The wedding planner? Why would she be writing to you at your office? The pastor promised she didn't charge for her services. Is it a bill? Maybe she sends all the couples she helped a bill and doesn't let the church know about it. Boy, I didn't expect that."

"It's not a bill. It's a suicide note. Listen to this. 'I killed Earl because he found out about Eddie's affair and thought he was being a good Christian by telling me about it. He brought horrible shame on me. Now the whole world will know. I'd rather be dead, and it's his fault. We were fine. Vernice.'"

"That's amazing. Are you sure it's from Vernice? It doesn't sound like her at all."

"You knew her better than I did. Was Eddie having an affair such an embarrassment to her she would kill herself and make her boys grow up without a mother?"

From the moment I met Vernice, she bragged incessantly about how perfect her husband and children were. The face she presented to the public was very important to her, but had it been at the price of her kids? Why would she work so hard to present the perfect family to everyone and then reveal everything wrong with her life, to be published in the newspaper?

"The paper is going to publish the letter after the police department gives the okay."

"Did she write it by hand?"

"It's typed."

"Then it's hard to be sure if she actually wrote it, mailed it, and then killed herself. I mean, most people leave a note near where they kill themselves, right?"

"I thought so."

A few minutes later, after I rejoined the shower and opened the gifts from the Camden Chapel ladies, I pulled Mary and Ellie aside to tell them the news of the note.

"What do you think?"

Mary shrugged. "Because it's typed, we may never know. Anyone could have typed it up and mailed it to Ben."

Ellie shook her head. "Those poor kids. They went to camp, and they had a mother. By the time it was over, they were motherless."

Everything was changing. We now knew Earl was drugged and pushed off the belfry, and now we had Vernice leaving a suicide note because her husband had an affair. Not only did she write the note, but she also sent it to the newspaper, where it would be published.

After all the endless days I had spent with her hearing about her perfect home life, I knew she would never write that note. Even though the Bible says pride cometh before a fall, I didn't see Vernice forgetting her pride or letting her habit of complimenting herself go by the wayside. She absolutely loved herself, and people who love themselves do not destroy the thing they worship.

It was not suicide. Vernice was murdered. What wasn't clear to me, though, was who had so much to lose they had to murder her. Had it been her husband, trying to get free of his talkative wife who insisted on wearing floral dresses that no longer fit? Was it the woman Eddie was sleeping with in sleazy motels every weekend, and could that woman possibly be Davita?

How strange was it that there were two suspicious deaths within the same congregation in a period of two weeks? What scared me most was bad things often came in threes, and my wedding was next on the Camden Chapel church calendar.

I needed to know more about Eddie and whoever his mystery woman was. With that information, I might figure out who killed Vernice. If it wasn't suicide, then I had half the town to look at in her case. From the people she rubbed elbows with, managing weddings, to anyone she crossed. It could be a long list.

Chapter Twenty

As I helped clean up after the combined showers, my mind was reeling with the words of Vernice's supposed suicide note. Leslie stood next to me, wrapping leftover petit fours with plastic wrap.

"You two are now well equipped for your little home," she said, pulling the wrap perfectly tight from the edges.

"Thank you so much for putting together the church shower and then moving it to the library."

"When Davita announced to the group you were trying to go to both showers and not insult anyone, we all decided the best thing we could do was come to the library."

"It all came out perfect because of that. Thank you."

"Dot, are you going to carry a few of these boxes?" Aunt Mavis asked from the doorway. She had been toting our gifts back and forth and looked a little winded.

"Yes, of course. I'll be right there."

I grabbed one of my new Tupperware containers and started stacking sandwiches in it. Mary was helping Aunt Mavis, and when she came in for another load, I stopped her.

"Mary, take these sandwiches home for John and the kids."

Mary grinned. "Thank you! I'd love to take them home. Are you sure you want to put them in your new Tupperware? These babies have some solid burping lids."

"Yes," I laughed. "Just don't wear them out."

"I think most of the stuff is in the car, so I'll grab the sandwiches and head home. Thanks."

"No, thank you. I really appreciate you coming, and thank you for the afghan you crocheted for us. We'll put it on the back of the couch."

"Every house needs one for afternoon naps and snuggling in front of the television." She hugged me, picked up her container of sandwiches, and waved goodbye.

I turned back to Leslie. Maybe she could tell me something about Vernice that would help me to understand the suicide note sent to Ben at the paper. I had to be missing something about the woman. "How well did you know Vernice?"

"Oh, I don't know. As well as you can know anybody at church. She was one of those who came every Sunday, rain or shine. She also came to ladies' events when she had time. She tried to control those boys of hers, but it didn't always work out. We caught one of them peeing against the back wall of the church at Vacation Bible School one year. Not a major infraction, and boys will be boys, but Ben would never have done anything like that. She could be bossy, but for the most part, she filled a vital role at Camden Chapel."

"Did she ever seem low? You know, low enough to commit suicide?"

Leslie gave a quick shake of her head and frowned. "She wouldn't do that. I already told you she was at church every Sunday. Committing suicide is breaking a commandment. Her faith and her expectations of the life beyond this one were too strong. I just don't see it."

"You're right. A devout person has a lot to lose when they consider suicide. Can you tell me about Earl? Was there anyone at church he made angry enough to kill him?"

She clucked her tongue. "Earl was a well-meaning man, but..." she paused.

"But?"

"But not everyone wanted his advice, and no matter what secrets they were trying to keep, he'd find out. Not only that, but sometimes his discretion was questionable. We all know that was why our other organist, Cleta Offmeir, left. He told anyone who would listen that she bought her homemade stollen at the German bakery in Dallas. He found the box when he emptied the trash.

She walked right out between services on a Sunday morning."

I thought back to my few moments with Earl. He seemed so kind, even grandfatherly. In this age of realizing a woman can do anything a man can do, it occurred to me a man, no matter how harmless he looked, could gossip. Earl was a gossip. His sense of right and wrong was amplified from years of police training, but discretion didn't seem to be a part of the curriculum.

"We were lucky to get her replaced so quickly. Pastor Ross put an ad in the Dallas paper, and we had Charlotte by the next Sunday. She used to play organ at an Episcopalian church, and lucky for us, they sing the same hymns. Replacing Cleta that quickly made her even more angry at all of us. I hear she's worshiping in Fort Worth now. I guess it's worth the drive to be somewhere they don't have ex-policemen watching your every move." She stopped talking for a moment and then let out a gasp. "Oh, you're playing investigative lady, aren't you? This is so exciting. You'll have to share all the information you uncover with Ben so he can solve the case!"

Ouch. "Yes, I will. Thanks, Leslie."

Aunt Mavis and my mother stood in the doorway, arms intertwined. "Well, my dear, you have successfully delegated the job of loading the car," Mom said.

"But we'll leave unpacking it all at your new house to you. I'm tired," Aunt Mavis said. "We're heading over to the community pool to dip our toes in the water. Half the kiddies are out school shopping, so it ought to be nice."

"Yes, and there are only a few more days until it closes for the year, so we're going swimming."

"I think that sounds like a great idea," I said to my mother. "It's so good you are doing something for yourselves. Thank you for everything today, both of you."

"You only get married once," my mother said.

"Yes. That's what I keep hearing. What about Ellie? Did she go home?"

"No. She's still here. She's upstairs going through Dr. Spock's baby and childcare book," Mavis said.

"I didn't know that was still in print. I used that," Mom said.

"She worried for nine months about the pregnancy, but now the real worrying begins. How to raise a kid. Now that's a lifetime dealio," Aunt Mavis said flatly.

I loved how Aunt Mavis put things. No one else would even dream of saying "dealio," but she was confident molding words to fit her needs.

Mavis handed me my keys. "Good luck with hauling it all out of your car. Get Ben to help you."

"I will."

After they left, I made my way upstairs, where Ellie had the Dr. Spock book as well as three others opened and spread across the library table. She looked pale and overwhelmed.

"My God, Dot. There's so much to learn here. When it comes to babies, I'm pretty well an idiot."

"Ellie, no, you're not."

"Did you know that if you don't get enough gas out of the baby by burping him, he can explode?"

"Explode? I've never heard of that."

She rushed over and picked up a book and quickly paged to a baby throwing up a stream of formula in a straight line across a room. "It's called projectile vomiting."

"Really? Babies vomit like laser beams?"

"Yes." She nodded solemnly. "I should have started reading these books the minute I found out I was pregnant. I'm so behind."

"You'll be fine. My mother did it. Your mother did it. You will do it. Now, I'm heading over to the rental house to drop off all the gifts. Would you like to come with me?" I glanced at the table. "That is, if you don't want to sit here and scare yourself some more."

Ellie started closing up books. "Sounds like a good idea. I'll just check these out. Besides, I don't think I want to be alone at the house."

"Why?"

"Remember what I told you about being followed? I know it sounded crazy, but I think it's still happening. Not just when I'm walking, but I keep seeing this beat-up, maroon-looking car around."

"Maybe you should tell the police."

"That seems a little much. They'll take one look at me and say I'm being dramatic. No, I'm still making sure I'm actually being followed and not imagining it."

"Well then, you can follow me in your car to my house. I'll look around to see if I see the maroon car following both of us."

When we got to the house, I waited for Ellie to come up the drive. "Sorry, Ellie. I didn't see anyone. Did you?"

"No. I didn't either. Maybe it is all in my mind."

"You go in and sit down, and I'll start bringing things in, okay?"

"Gladly," she said.

I started hauling in different items, leaving things in the kitchen mostly. When I got to Mary's afghan, I decided to place it on the back of the couch, but instead I found Ellie fast asleep, a baby book on her midsection. This was one of those moments I wished I had a camera. She was so sweet and only weeks away from becoming a mother. Her life would never be the same.

I folded the afghan and set it on the end of the couch. When I returned to the driveway for one more load, I saw it. The back end of a maroon sedan driving down the street. She was right. Someone *was* following her.

Chapter Twenty-One

We were one day from the wedding. Ben was finally off work for the wedding and honeymoon, and with everything going on, it couldn't be a minute sooner. The newspaper office was bustling from not only two local deaths but also a suicide note sent directly to Ben, so leaving to get married had been tough. I was experiencing mixed feelings. I was happy the wedding day was almost here, but I was also terrified the wedding day was almost here. Meanwhile, I tried not to look at today's date on the calendar. Friday the 13th was a silly superstition. I had to keep telling myself that. It felt like I had been spinning plates in the air for months, but Ben's only duties for the day were to pick up his black suit from the cleaners, complete with a tie, white shirt, and spit-shined black shoes. This evening, he would be going to a bachelor party being thrown for him by Al at the Uphill Bar. Friday the 13th is just another day, and it would not affect things any more than any other day of the year. I kept telling myself everything would be fine both today and tomorrow.

Ellie and I were dropping in at Lily's of the Field to look at our bouquets for the next day and to write a check for the bill. Because Lily's shop was new in town and trying to get traction, she gave us a discount, which really helped. Use of the church was free, and some of the food for the reception was being provided by the members. Ellie donated her services for the wedding dress, and Ben already had the suit. My parents were paying for the flowers, and Ben and I were paying for the honeymoon. I suppose it was what you would call a frugal wedding, but with me not working, it was just the right price for us. I needed to make sure that I properly thanked Lily for being so generous.

When we walked into the flower shop, we found Lily with her head in the cool case. "I put these here for you two. I saw you pull up."

I couldn't help but notice there were circles under her eyes. Had she been crying? Was seeing her high school sweetheart get married to another woman more important to her than she had let on in our earlier conversation?

I glanced at the beautifully shaped bouquet of daisies and marigolds. "These are stunning. You are quite the artist," I said.

"Have other people used them in bouquets?"

Lily, whose bottom lip was colored with a deep red lipstick, bit down on it thoughtfully. "It's the flower of the year, but as pretty as they are, they can lose those big petals with very little movement."

My bouquet was held together with florist tape and had a small handle underneath for me to put my hands through.

"How did you learn to do this?"

"Oh, you know. My first job was in a florist shop, and the florist trained me how to make the floral arrangements that were ordered frequently. It got to the point where I could throw them together quickly, and I moved on to sprays and casket blankets. I found that not only was I good at making floral arrangements, but I also understood the business end of managing a store. It took me a couple of years and a small loan from a friend, but I opened my own shop."

"You're an inspiration," Ellie said, stepping in front of the mirror and holding her bouquet on top of the baby she carried. "Tell me, does this bouquet make me look fat?"

I burst out laughing, and after a second, Lily joined me.

"Yes," I said, trying to catch my breath. "I think it puts on ten pounds."

"For sure," Lily agreed. "I knew I shouldn't use those Gerber daisies. Such big petals."

Ellie snorted, and we laughed until she begged us to stop, as it could cause an accident before she could get to the bathroom.

I gasped for breath. "I think I needed that."

Lily's bottom lip trembled as she wiped a tear from one eye after laughing so hard. "Me too. It's been a rough week."

"Tell me about it," Ellie said. "My back hurts. My ankles are swollen, and I can't wear shoes with laces because I can't reach my feet. How about you, Dot? What's your body count up to?"

Only Ellie could get away with gallows humor, and I laughed again, then leaned on a shelf made out of mirrors, knocking over an arrangement of mums. It crashed to the floor, scattering flowers and broken mirror pieces across the store. "I'm so sorry." I felt terrible breaking something in Lily's flower shop. She was trying to start a business, and I was wrecking the place.

"I thought I was the clumsy one," Ellie said under her breath.

"Oh my. I knew I shouldn't have put that there. Let me get a broom." Lily ran to the backroom.

"Not wanting to state the obvious, but you just broke a mirror on Friday the 13th," Ellie whispered.

"Thanks for reminding me. Just what I wanted to hear the day before my wedding."

"That's what cousins are for."

Lily returned, broom and dustpan in hand. I continued to apologize. "I'm so sorry."

"Don't worry about it. I break things all the time," she assured me.

I first came to the flower shop all wrapped up in Lily's past, but suddenly I wanted to know about her present. What was her life like now? What did she do when she wasn't arranging flowers? "I know all about what's happening in my life, Lily. What's going on with you? You said you'd had a rough week. I mean, if you feel comfortable sharing with us. I know you don't know me, but I'd like to get to know you."

Lilly gave a quick shake of her head. "That's nice. I would like to get to know you. After all, you are the girl who stole Ben's heart." She stopped for a minute, then said, "Not from me, of course. So, my life is kind of complicated, and things are changing for me. Let's just say my Prince Charming is turning into a toad real fast. I'm not sure if I did the right thing moving my shop here." She shook her head quickly as if to shake off the thought. "You don't need to hear my troubles the day before your wedding to Ben. Let's just say, I wish I had made some better choices a while back."

Lily's words were cryptic, but I didn't feel comfortable asking any more than what she had just revealed. I had to think she wished she had never let Ben go all those years ago. Especially if the man she was with now was proving to be a disappointment.

"Ben had a lot of trouble telling me he asked you to marry him, and I'll admit it made me jealous," I confessed.

Lily looked out the window at the street, her eyes following the slow passing of the cars. "You don't have to worry about me. Ben is hook, line, and sinker for you, not me."

"I know that now, and I have to say I'm glad I met you. I know you're delivering the flowers to the church tomorrow, but could you also come to the wedding? We'd both love to have you there."

"Oh, I couldn't do that. I mean, how bad does it look for the old girlfriend to show up at a wedding?"

"Think of it this way. You're the old girlfriend, but to us, you are a new friend. But it would be really nice if you wore an ugly dress. You seem to look good in everything," Ellie suggested not too subtly.

A tear slid down Lily's cheek. "I don't know. I guess I'll think about it."

"Good."

"I'll put the bouquets in the cooler and bring them tomorrow when I deliver the rest of the flowers. That way they will be fresh," Lily said.

"Yes! That would be one less thing to worry about," I said. I produced the payment and laid it on the counter. "I'll see you tomorrow then."

"I'm looking forward to it," she said.

I handed back the bouquet, and one of the petals drifted slowly to the floor. Lily looked a little less sad, and I hoped I hadn't just made a mistake inviting her to the wedding. I still wasn't sure if she was in love with Ben, and I could be making things worse for her.

As we walked out into the sunlight, Ellie whispered. "You did well. It's not like Lily is unattractive. I don't know if I could have invited her to my wedding if she was pining for Al."

"I'm having a few second thoughts, but I kind of think Ben would have wanted me to invite her. He still speaks fondly of her, although he's assured me that the romance is long over."

"Well, if it isn't Ben she looks sad about, who is it?"

"Exactly. We need to think better of her. Just because she's sexier than Sophia Loren, that doesn't mean she's in some torrid affair. Maybe her parakeet died."

"She doesn't look like the kind of woman who needs a parakeet to keep her from being lonely."

"Now, that's an unfair view of her, just because she's pretty. Gorgeous people get lonely too." Ellie pulled a paper fan out of her large handbag and began to push at the hot air with it. When I tried to get into the breeze she was creating, I noticed Charlotte standing about half a block away. She was talking to a guy who looked straight out of *Rebel Without a Cause*. His hair was slicked into a pompadour, and he wore a black leather jacket on top of a white shirt. How could he stand that jacket in this sweltering heat?

"Turn around slowly and look down the street," I said in a low voice.

Ellie jerked her head around, perfectly contrary to what I told her. "What am I looking at?" she whispered back.

"Isn't that Charlotte from Camden Chapel, and could that be her boyfriend with her?" I searched my memory. "What's his name? Mac. That was it."

Ellie's eyes narrowed in on the pair. "Hmmm, if he is, I don't see that congregation feeling comfortable around a guy like that."

"You are so right. If Vernice had laid eyes on him, she would have let everyone know. Let's go talk to them." Before we could get a foot farther, the two walked around the corner.

"Maybe they saw us looking at them," Ellie said. "They had to."

"I told you to turn around slowly," I reminded her. Charlotte had talked about her boyfriend, but not much, only about his lack of commitment. Now that I had seen him, I needed to reevaluate her and her alibi.

We turned back to the car. Lily was standing in front of the window, a tissue in hand, wiping away a tear.

"She is so beautiful, but so sad," Ellie whispered.

Lily placed the mum I had knocked over, which was now in a new vase, on a pedestal in the front window display, then turned back into the store.

We had both attended school in Camden at the same time, but in different schools. It was amazing how you could grow up in the same environment as another person but never meet them. There were other kids around at the movies and town events like Fourth of July parades, but I always stayed with my friends from my school. I had never seen Ben until I met him at that fateful town meeting on a stormy night two years ago. It was funny that now that I was older and getting married, I didn't consider a single female friend from that time to be my maid of honor. The girl I was always closest to was Ellie. Some of them and their families would be at the wedding, and I certainly didn't have any old boyfriends I wanted to invite.

"This is going to sound strange, but even though I was ready to be insanely jealous of Lily, I'm finding I really like her. Is that weird?"

"No, not with your heart. You're a good person, and you can also recognize goodness in others," Ellie said, placing her hand on her midsection. She held her breath for a moment and then let it out.

"More Braxton Hicks?"

"Yes. They're driving me crazy, but it's a healthy sign that the baby is coming. By the way, sorry about Al missing his appointment with you the other day. All he can think about is the baby. Sometimes I think he's worse than I am."

"Yeah, that's okay. You know, I've been thinking the same thing about Ben and the wedding details. He's so nervous, and it all has to do with him wanting to please his parents."

"Now that we're talking about Al and Ben, we need to go check on Al. He's getting ready for the bachelor party at the Uphill Bar. Could we go there next?"

"What is there to prepare for a bachelor party at a bar? The men show up, and the bartender brings them beer."

Ellie gave me a sly smile. "That's what they tell us, but we don't really know for sure, now do we? How many bachelor parties have you attended?"

"None."

She snapped her fingers. "Exactly! I wonder if they'll try to hire a stripper."

I hadn't thought of that and was surprised it was just occurring to me.

"Where would they find a stripper around here?"

"There's a place in Fort Worth called The Cellar. Girls wait tables in bikinis, and sometimes they strip for tips. It's scandalous. It came out in the Warren Report that John Kennedy's Secret Service guys were there the night before the assassination. It was all over the news. You never knew about that?"

"No." Ellie was surprising to me sometimes. "You read the Warren Report?"

"Hey, I'm not just a pretty face. Well, to be truthful about it, parts of it were in the paper. I saw it there."

"In Fort Worth? So close."

"Yes, and now I'm just wondering if they deliver."

I laughed. "Just another reason why we need to check on Al."

Chapter Twenty-Two

When we got to the bar, there were only a few cars and Al's pickup in the parking lot. It was still a little early in the day for Camden drinkers. Sunlight sliced through the darkness when we opened the door from the street, illuminating swirling motes of airborne grit dancing above the worn linoleum floor. The air hung thick with the mingled scents of stale beer, cigarette smoke, and something vaguely fried. The walls were adorned with a haphazard collection of Lone Star beer signs and faded black-and-white photos of local football heroes. A handful of patrons occupied the mismatched collection of vinyl-covered stools and wobbly wooden tables.

The jukebox itself was gleaming chrome and neon, its glass face displaying rows of 45s, but the music was a twangy lament of a country song drifting from a small transistor radio perched precariously on the bar.

Al leaned against the dark mahogany bar, writing something on a crinkled sheet of paper. Next to him was a tall man, probably weighing in at over 200 pounds. He was holding a Lone Star beer, and when his eyes lit on me, he smiled. He started to come forward, but Ellie interrupted.

"Hey, Al," Ellie said as she waddled into the darkened bar.

Al looked up suddenly. "Is the baby coming?" He started to fold up the paper, ready to rush out the door. The man next to him smiled but backed away.

Ellie shook her head. "Settle down. No, the baby isn't coming. If the baby was coming, I wouldn't be this relaxed. I'd be screaming my fool head off. No, I just came over to see how you were doing before the big stag party."

Al breathed out a sigh of relief and ran his hand over his forehead. "Don't do this to me, woman. I'm already jumping out of my skin that our young'un will come and I'll miss it somehow."

He then noticed me. "Hey, Dot. Nice to see you."

The large man next to Al extended a hand. "I finally get to meet the girl I've heard so much about. Dot Morgan, the secretary who solves murders. I'm Dusty Warner, Ben's old roommate." He then turned to Ellie. "And you, madame, are about to pop."

Ellie rolled her eyes. "Ben never told us how observant you are of the obvious."

"Sorry, Ben always says I talk before I think. I didn't mean to offend you. When is your baby due?"

Al took a folded handkerchief out of his back pocket and wiped it across his forehead. "Any day. It's like waiting for an alarm clock to ring. It's killing me."

So, this was the fabled Dusty. There was a slight crinkle in the corners of his eyes, and his gaze held a softness. He was looking at me in a friendly way, as if wanting to know the woman his former roommate was marrying. "It's so nice to meet you. Ben told me that you were a part of the team that opened the Astrodome down in Houston?"

Dusty beamed with pride. "Yes, ma'am. I certainly was. It was a big deal. Did you know that I was the one who came up with the idea to make the grounds crew wear space suits? Yep, that was me."

"I didn't know that."

"Yep. The Astrodome is a thing of the future, and with that little touch, it was perfect," he said.

"Does Ben know you're here?" I asked.

"Yes. I went to his office, and he told me to come over here to help Al, but he seems to have everything ready. I'm mostly just day drinking and playing the jukebox."

"Pace yourself, man," Al said. "You don't want to be snoring when the party starts."

"Of course," Dusty said. "But it's a hot day, and these Lone Star beer signs got to me."

I drew closer to Al. "Ellie told me there was a possibility you might be hiring some form of entertainment. Now, I'm pretty sure you're not going for a clown or setting up pony rides, so I have to ask, you aren't ordering in a stripper from The Cellar, are you?"

A series of wrinkles lined Al's forehead. "Now, why would she say a foolish thing like that?"

"Did I just hear you call the mother of your child a fool? Did I?" Ellie said.

Al looked overwhelmed. "No, dear. Not at all. Why don't you have a seat? All this standing is not good for you."

"I'm pretty sure the baby won't just drop out." Ellie walked over to a chair and sat down. "Don't mind if I do. Of course, now I'm staring at the beer sign."

"Let me get you something cold to drink, honey." Al held up a finger. "Can I get an ice water?"

The bartender, a large man named Cal, reached for a glass, scooped in some ice, and prepared a tall glass of water. "Here you go." He handed it across the bar to Al, who then delivered it to Ellie.

"You are a wonderful husband, Al," I said.

"Thank you. I've got to take care of my girl. As far as strippers, I wouldn't know how to ask. I'm just a small-town Texas boy, and those, uh, ladies are out of my league."

Dusty took a sip of beer and then said, "I hear they are open to new clientele if a guy has the proper financing."

"And that's the next problem. Something like that costs too much, and boy howdy. Why would I want to get Ben in trouble the night before his wedding? He has the rest of his marriage for getting in trouble. Just look at me, a living example. Nope, this is my job. Have a nice little party, drink a few beers, maybe tell a blue story or two, and then get him home to his parents' house."

Ellie drank from the water. "You worry too much, Al. And from what I hear, Ben is starting to do the same thing with this wedding. When you get him here tonight, make him loosen up. He's as tight as the lid on a mayonnaise jar right now."

"I'll do my best," Al said. "Why is he so worried? It's pretty obvious he's marrying the prettiest girl in town."

"Here, here," Dusty said, raising his beer.

Ellie harumphed. Al quickly amended his comment. "Prettiest single girl in town. I have the prettiest married girl."

My frustration with Ben's parents started spilling out. "Ben's worried because of his mother. He is afraid if he doesn't do everything exactly right, she'll be upset. I don't know all the details, but I think it has to do with his aunt? His mother has ideas of how things should be, and the aunt didn't live her life the same way."

"You know, now that you say it, that makes a lot of sense," Dusty added. "When we roomed together, every time his mom came for a visit, he made me help him clean our dorm room. I'll admit back in those days I was pretty messy; hell, we both were, but he didn't seem to care except when his parents were going to visit. I don't know what I was expecting, but she was nice when she got there. Didn't run any white-gloved hands over a single thing. I think the guy worries too much. Of course, he would tell you I don't worry enough. I have a job I love, and I'm a pretty happy guy. What is there to worry about?"

Al patted him on the back. "You are absolutely right, brother. I used to be like that, but now that I'm about to be a daddy, I worry more than I ever have, and I have this love for a baby I haven't even met yet. Is that crazy?"

"Oh, Al," Ellie said, a tear misting her eye. "You're making me cry."

"It's true. When I met Ellie, I thought I understood unconditional love, but now with little Al, Jr. coming, it's increased tenfold. Whatever Ben is worrying about, he shouldn't. Parents love their kids no matter what they've done. Even if it's a horrible thing, there's a little part of them that will still love that baby boy they gave birth to."

"Al, that is so sweet. You need to share all of this with Ben tonight. Maybe it will help him to stop trying to be such a parent pleaser," I suggested.

"So, you're marrying a man who wants to always please his parents, but I think you have some of the same qualities. It's probably what attracted you to each other. Don't you always want to make your parents happy?" Ellie asked.

I thought of my mother. "It's not about making them happy right now as much as letting them down. Getting married is changing things between me and my mother. I won't be her little girl anymore."

Ellie put her glass on the table. "I wouldn't worry about that, Dot. She'll adjust. My mother, besides being relieved I finally landed a man, found a whole new set of things to boss me around about. It's like she evolved into the married daughter/grandma-to-be model. Yes, she'll never stop finding ways to tell me how to do things. It's a gift."

Having Aunt Mavis as a mother could be difficult, I agreed, but she was a person I always wanted in my life. "Your mother is a gift. It's just she's wrapped in burlap, not wrapping paper."

"Cheers to that," Ellie said, lifting her water glass.

"Cheers," Dusty repeated.

Al picked up the paper he had been writing on. "I'm trying to help Dusty here write his best man speech for the wedding reception, but I don't think I'm any good at this. Any suggestions, Dot?"

The wedding reception. That seemed like years away at this point. "All the other toasts I've heard usually start out with some sort of funny, embarrassing story and end up with a really nice, heartfelt thing. People usually cry by the end."

Al put a hand on his chin and squinted at the paper. "Cry? I don't want to make anyone cry now. That doesn't seem right."

"Crying is good, Al. Happy tears show how much people love one another," Ellie said, but then she jumped and put her hand on her baby.

"Is the baby coming?" Al said for the second time.

Ellie breathed in and then out slowly. "No, Al. It's Braxton Hicks. Calm down."

"Easy for you to say," he muttered.

"Man, the anxiety level in this town is through the roof," Dusty muttered. "I think I'll put another dime in the jukebox."

Chapter Twenty-Three

When I was a little girl, I always dreamed of my wedding day, and it had finally arrived. I imagined looking very grown up when I walked down the aisle, sun streaming through the windows, casting a pearly light on everything. Everyone in the pews would turn and look at me and smile. My father would hold my arm, and my mother would cry from the front pew as the music played softly in the background. At the altar would be a man who closely resembled Rock Hudson or maybe Paul Newman, and he would be astounded at the perfect woman walking toward him.

The day was here, and it was nothing like I had imagined. It was real. No music. No Paul Newman, and I could hear thunder outside. I wasn't sure if I was happy or just terrified and mistaking the butterflies for joy. Anyone who has ever wished for love waits for this special day. A day when Cinderella marries her prince, when love is the word of the day, and when, essentially, life goes on. I guess I expected sparkles and little birds flying to my uplifted hand as I sang out in a ludicrously high voice about my prince. In reality, I woke up to an apartment that was more empty than full, a wedding dress hanging off my closet door, and a feeling of creeping apprehension. Was I really doing this? Did I really want to be with one person for the rest of my life? I had been pretty happy being one in a two-by-two world. I pulled the sheet up over my head, willing my brain to stop sowing seeds of fear and doubt.

I tried to replace the worries with positive thoughts. This was the power of positive thinking. First, people who come together as a couple are so often stronger in this world. That worked. Then thoughts of relationships I had witnessed lately weren't giving me any confidence in long-lasting wedded bliss. There was Vernice and Eddie, who were hiding infidelity, but then I'd also seen Charlotte and her boyfriend, who couldn't make a commitment even though they had been engaged for five years. Granted, they did look like they were happy together. Had their relationship made them stronger? Of course, I couldn't go down this rabbit hole without thinking of good and loving couples in my life. Ellie and Al were such a loving partnership, and now preparing to welcome a baby, and my own parents still loved each other after so many years. Yes. Being in a marriage would be okay for me and Ben. I had to keep thinking that.

I picked up my wristwatch from the cardboard box that was serving as my bed table. A panic ran through me. It was almost 8:30. I had fallen asleep with my window open, and the smell of rain was in the air. I should have been out of bed an hour ago. I was already late on my wedding day. Ellie was supposed to have come by at eight and wake me up. It was one thing for *me* to be late, but I never would have expected both of us to oversleep. It was not like her to forget something like that, especially today. I jumped out of bed and put on the clothes I had laid out the day before. Maybe she had gone into labor, and no one had time to call me? What if it was something worse than that? What if she had gone into labor at home alone last night while Al was at the bachelor party? I needed to get to her right away. I brushed my teeth, grabbed my keys, my wedding dress still in plastic, an additional bag of shoes, my makeup case, and the daisy headband I would wear instead of a traditional veil. With all of that, I attempted to take the stairs two at a time, causing my landlady, Arlene, to look up from the kitchen as I passed her.

"Is everything okay? I thought you'd be up hours ago," she asked as she stood in her bathrobe, hair in curlers, while pressing the front of a light green summer dress. "If you didn't get up by nine, I was going to wake you up."

"No. Ellie was supposed to be here."

"Whatever in the world would make her late on a day like today?" The iron hissed as she set it on its base.

"I have to go check on her."

"Then let me carry some of that." Arlene took the makeup case and the daisy headband and followed me as I stepped outside, the screen door slamming behind us as we walked into a muggy, overcast day. It was one of those days where a person felt anxious just waiting for the rain to break the humidity. I was anxious enough as it was.

I pulled up to Ellie's house and ran up the sidewalk. As I jumped onto the wraparound porch, I could hear Ellie's voice through the screen door. "Yes, but he never came home. Are you sure you have no idea where he might have gone after the bachelor party?"

I let myself in and sat next to Ellie, who had stretched out the phone cord to the living room chair where she was sprawled out, the baby at the highest point of her position.

"Okay, thank you. Let me know if you hear anything."

She lumbered up and returned the phone to the wall in the kitchen. "Al didn't come home last night."

"He didn't?"

"No, and before you ask, I already called Ben's parents' house. The groom came home around one. I still don't have any details about the party. What could have happened that Al didn't come home?"

Hearing Ben had made it to his parents' house was a relief. I had begun to have visions of standing at the altar by myself and then felt selfish thinking of Ben when Ellie is worrying over her missing husband. Al was like the slogan for a Timex watch. "Takes a licking and keeps on ticking." He was the most dependable person I knew.

Even though it was out of character for him, I had to ask. "Do you think maybe he had too much to drink and passed out somewhere?"

Ellie placed a hand on the baby growing inside of her. "It has to be something like that, but you know Al and I dated for years before we married. This is not like him. He isn't a heavy drinker."

"Exactly. Maybe he drank more than he normally does and couldn't handle it." I glanced at my watch. "We need to get over to the church. We have to do hair and makeup."

Ellie put a hand to her forehead. "Oh, Dot. I'm so sorry. I was supposed to pick you up. Let me get my bag."

After a few minutes, we were off to the church where I would be getting married. I was nervous and worried, and so far, it was nothing like my dream.

Chapter Twenty-Four

When we burst through the door of the room set aside for us at the Camden Chapel, all the women I loved were in various states of beauty treatments. My mother, Aunt Mavis, and Mary Oliva each looked relieved to see us.

We decided to all prepare together at the church at the suggestion of my mother. "Let's share these final moments before Dot gets married together," she had said. We all agreed it would be fun to get made up together and put on our dresses. Several of the ladies had small makeup cases that came with their luggage, which sat upright and contained a mirror. Between that and the portable hair dryers, we decided we would become a temporary house of beauty.

I received my makeup case when I turned sixteen and was going to Dallas for a debate tournament. It was a sky-blue Samsonite cosmetic case with gathered blue silk pockets that lined the sides, and a mirror mounted to the top lid. I remember laying out my makeup, what little I was allowed to wear at sixteen, and then my shampoo and lotion. I felt like a grown woman carrying around my little blue bag, just like Grace Kelly in *Rear Window*.

"You made it! We were about to send the police out for a welfare check," my mother said.

Mary smiled. "She's not kidding about that. What kept you?"

In the other corner of the room stood Leslie and a woman I didn't recognize. Because this room was used for an early elementary Sunday school room, the tables were very low to the ground, flanked by an assortment of tiny chairs. Leslie and her guest stood next to a bulletin displaying Zacchaeus and the infamous tree he hid in, a traditional Bible story. There was a silence between us, and then Leslie stepped forward. "Glad you made it. We were getting worried you were planning on leaving Ben at the altar." She gestured to the other woman. "This is my sister Joanie."

"Aunt Joanie? It's nice to meet you. Ben's talked about you." I stepped forward to take her hands. She was slightly taller than Ben's mother, Leslie, and she wasn't quite as polished. She wore a thick silver watch on her wrist, and her hair was also short, but with no bouffant hair spray holding it up. Instead of pumps, she wore a more standard shoe I had seen on older women, although she wasn't much older than my own mother.

"I hope it wasn't all bad," Joanie said. "I'm kind of the black sheep of the family, you know."

Leslie stepped forward. "That's not true, and you know it, Joanie. We love everybody equally in our family."

Joanie smiled. "Of course we do." She turned back to me. "I'm just so happy to finally meet you. Anybody that makes my nephew Ben this happy, and a little goofy I might add, is aces in my book." Then she pulled me forward and hugged me a little harder than I expected from a woman I had just met. It was different, but it was so genuine I hugged her back.

"May I ask what kept you?" Leslie asked.

"Well, first I overslept, but also there's more. Ellie can't find Al."

Mavis pulled off the vinyl cap of the white plastic hair dryer she had brought from home. "What do you mean you can't find Al? That's crazy. Al is always where he's supposed to be."

"I know, Mom, but he threw Ben's bachelor party last night and hasn't been heard from since."

"Must have been some party," my mother said. "Oh dear, I hope they didn't hire any…entertainment."

Ellie shook her head from side to side. "Al promised they weren't doing that kind of thing. He made it sound like a simple get-together where a bunch of men drank beer and told stories. Sort of the male equivalent to the wedding shower, just the groom gets beer instead of Tupperware."

Mavis nodded. "One time during the war, we had a little party to celebrate one of the men having a new baby stateside. It was a wild one. The next day, the guy was AWOL. We found him later dead in a Jeep. He must have fallen off the roof, or maybe he jumped and broke his neck on the steering wheel."

Ellie paled, and I wanted to thwack Aunt Mavis over the head. Didn't she realize the fuel she just threw on her daughter's fear?

Mary came over and stood in front of Ellie, a warmth in her voice. "I didn't hear anything from the station, so it's nothing bad, I'm sure."

"Then where is he?" Ellie asked as she stepped behind a folding screen Aunt Mavis had left over from her nursing days.

"He'll show up. They always do. Maybe he's asleep in his truck. Have you tried looking for his vehicle?" Mary asked patiently, showing that she was used to working with frantic people at the police department.

"Those bachelor parties never turn out well, in my opinion," Leslie said.

Joanie attempted to sit in one of the child-sized chairs. "I heard they were a lot of fun."

Ellie came out from behind the screen, now wearing her blue matron of honor gown. She reached for a tissue in a conveniently placed tissue box and then dabbed at her eyes. "No, I suppose we could take a swing by the bar."

"Sure," Mary reassured her. "You'll find him. Stuff like this is easy. We get cases like this all the time after bachelor parties. Eventually, the missing person wakes up with a terrible headache and a guilty conscience. He'll call, and if he doesn't, I'll help you find him. I wish figuring out who dumped the caretaker out of the belfry were that simple."

"Excuse me? Someone fell out of the belfry?" Joanie asked.

"Yes," Leslie said. "I'll fill you in later."

"Have you heard anything about any of the murders?" my mother asked.

"Sadly, no. Detective Barrerra is working on it, but we really don't have a clear suspect for Earl. He seemed like a nice guy to me. As for Vernice, they are looking closely at her husband. That affair he was having turned out to be the town's worst-kept secret."

Leslie gasped. "An affair? I had no idea. Poor Vernice. She never said a thing."

"Do they know who he's been having an affair with?" I asked, wondering about Davita. I had dismissed that theory just because of the fact that she didn't want kids, and he had two of them.

"No, but I think we're close," said Mary. "It had to be someone from out of town because no one reports seeing him out with anyone other than his wife here in Camden."

Someone from out of town? If that were the case, then I might be right, and Davita wasn't the mistress. Could it be a woman who worked at one of the construction companies he visited for his sales job? Having worked for a construction company once, I knew the existence of women in that world was small, and they were usually parked in an office or trailer somewhere. I slowly took the plastic off my wedding dress and was quickly accompanied by my mother, who started smoothing down the front. I turned to Mary. "When I met Vernice, I was pretty sure she had a life anyone would love to have. Now I'm not too sure."

"Can you blame her? We all present a face to the public that may or may not represent us. That's why they call them secrets," Mary said.

"I guess." I scanned the room to check on how Ellie was doing, but she wasn't there. "Where did Ellie go?" I asked.

Everyone looked around.

"That girl!" Aunt Mavis said. "She's gone to look for Al. Doesn't she know she can't go running off like that at eight and a half months pregnant?"

My mother's voice of reason cut in. "We just have to hope she makes it back in time."

"It is concerning her husband is missing, don't you think?" Leslie added.

There was a light knock on the door. Lily came in wearing a light pink dress with a pink rose corsage. It was a dramatic contrast to her coloring, and today she was stunning. "I brought the bouquets for you and Ellie," she said as she placed them on a bookcase. "I think you've got a good two to three hours before they wilt. I added a little something to keep them perky."

Leslie came forward. "Lily, it's so good to see you again. Ben told me you were back in town." She hugged the young florist. "I should have stopped by your flower shop to say hello, but we've all been so busy with the wedding. How are you, dear?"

Lily took a step back. "I'm fine. I'm so happy for Ben. I think he found a wonderful girl."

"Yes," Leslie grinned. "We have big hopes for their lives together."

I tried not to think about her hopes for our future and how different they were from my own.

Lily looked around and then back at me. "Where is your cousin? She didn't have the baby, did she?"

"We hope not," Mavis answered. "She'll probably be right back. She never goes too long without visiting the bathroom."

"Oh, well, I'll just leave these here for now. I need to check on some things in the sanctuary." Lily placed the bouquets on a shelf that held a series of little golden Bible stories and backed out of the room.

I went behind the folding screen and quickly changed into my wedding dress. It was a simple shift with cap sleeves and a very short skirt. Rising up from the hemline, Ellie had adorned it with white daisies sprinkled here and there across the skirt in a whimsical fashion. I pulled out the white knee-high boots that went with the dress and stepped into them, and then I pulled the daisy hairband out of my bag and stepped out.

My mother put her hands to her chest in prayer fashion. "Oh, Dot. It's adorable. You look…" Her eyes started to tear up. "You look…like my grown-up daughter. Here, let me put your hair up."

I sat awkwardly on the small chairs meant for five-year-olds as she pinned up my blond hair, letting a little swoop down as we had practiced in a mirror one day. After that, she placed the daisy headband in my hair.

"You look beautiful," Leslie said in a small voice.

I glanced in a full-length mirror that had been set out on its side along the wall. I had tried on the dress and headband together before in Bluebonnet's, but this time, this time was different. I looked different. Ellie had pulled off the look I wanted when I paged through *Bride's* magazine. It was unimaginable that I was getting married in the tiny town of Camden, Texas, when I looked like I was fresh off the runway in New York.

"You look like a bride," Aunt Mavis added.

My mother, now over her initial shock, wasn't quite as pleased as the other ladies. "My, that skirt is a little short, don't you think?"

We were all jolted out of our reverie when Clarence poked his head into the Sunday school room. "Sorry, ladies, but has anyone seen our organist? I'm trying to warm up the choir, and we have no accompanist."

I was in such a hurry to get into the church I hadn't stopped to notice there had been no music playing. Not even a practice session before the wedding, or the sound of Davita warming up her voice to a set of scales.

"I haven't seen her yet. Sometimes she steps out to smoke a cigarette."

Now the organist was late? Were we going to have to break out the kazoos and everyone hum along? How could all this be happening on my wedding day? I thought people had problems like drunk groomsmen, but never had I heard of people going missing. Al, Ellie, and now Charlotte?

"That woman," Clarence grumbled. "If she went off with her 'Rebel Without a Clue' boyfriend on a lark, I will personally see to it that she is fired as soon as your wedding is over. I swear, that man says, 'Jump,' and she says, 'How high?' Lord, save me from insecure women. Every time I talk to her, she's worried about losing him. She won't admit it, but she's older than he is, and the whole settle-down thing is a bit past her, if you know what I mean. Seriously, with that age gap, how could she see herself with him, starting a family? She wants the whole shebang. Husband, kids, white picket fence." He took off his glasses, polished them with his jacket lapel, and then said, "I'll have to see if Mrs. Owens can fill in." He looked at me. "I apologize in advance for the sour notes about to come your way, Miss Morgan."

For the first time since I started planning and made my first note in my notebook, I wished Vernice was here. She'd know just what to do. She'd probably have another accompanist on standby and have half the community out looking for Al.

"I never knew Charlotte wanted to start a family. Is that what she told you?" I asked.

"Oh yes. She said she would do just about anything to have a baby. You know she's in that age you women get in. Baby on the brain. Why do you think she's been knitting little blue sweaters? She's started a hope chest for the baby she doesn't even have."

A hope chest for a baby when she wasn't married or even in a place in her relationship to think about having a child in or out of marriage? Lots of women get maternal urges, but I didn't know any who had hope chests full of baby clothes. She had been so interested in Ellie's baby.

Charlotte.

How had I not seen it before? Could she be so desperate for a child she would be capable of hurting Ellie? I made myself stop. It was my wedding day. The worst possible day to run out and confront…I wasn't sure if I was overreacting. I tried to slow down my breathing and focus.

This was the place I wanted to be.

This was the day I had dreamed of since I was a little girl.

But Ellie was in trouble, and I wasn't sure just how much trouble. Maybe Ellie was out searching for Al, and that was all. She was searching for him and would come through the door on his arm in the next few minutes. I reached for an eyeliner on the table and started applying it. I was focused and ready to get married.

What if the person who took Al really wanted Ellie? Getting Al out of the way would make Ellie defenseless, especially in the state she was in. I added a little blush to my cheekbones. I was staying focused. Ben was waiting. All of our friends and family were waiting. This was it. The Big Show.

I turned to Mary. "Do you have your car with you?"

"John dropped me off early. He's at home getting the kids ready. Why?"

"Come with me." I grabbed Mary by the arm and started walking to the door.

My mother was talking to Ben's mother, but stopped abruptly when she saw me about to leave the room. "Dot? Where are you going?"

I didn't answer my mother as I ran down the hall wearing a white mini bridal gown with white boots, a really bad idea for Texas in August, but not important at the moment.

Leslie followed us out into the hallway. "Dot! What are you doing? Please don't tell me you're leaving. Not right now."

"I promise I'll be back," I shouted to her. "Mary, too."

"I'll make sure she gets back, Mrs. Morgan. Don't worry," Mary said as the light from the lobby hit us on the way out.

Leslie ran up the hall to stop us. "You can't do this. Your wedding is a little more than an hour away. There is nothing more important than right here, right now. Turn around, young lady."

Leslie Dalton looked panicked, and I was the sole reason. I should have stayed focused and worked on getting ready for my wedding, but I just couldn't stop myself. Not when it was Ellie. I turned to face her. "I think Ellie is in danger, and so is Al. Hold down the fort here for me. I'll explain it all when I get back."

We ran down the hall to the narthex while others were stirring in the sanctuary.

Leslie, who followed us, gestured to the sanctuary on our left. "Check and make sure she didn't show up. Maybe she's sitting at the organ right now, and you can stop all this silliness."

Mary nodded and stepped over to the closed sanctuary doors, and gently opening one, took a peek inside.

"Nope. There's no one at the organ. I do see Ben. He looks so handsome."

Leslie cut Mary off. "Dot, what are you doing? You can't just leave right now. You are about to marry my son." Her eyes were wide, and she crossed her arms as she prepared to stand her ground in front of the double doors.

"I promise, the thing I most want to do today is marry Ben, but you have to understand, I think my cousin Ellie is in mortal danger."

She shook her head, brow furrowed. "What are you talking about? How do you know this? All I see is a young woman running out the door on her wedding day. All I see is a girl who is about to break my son's heart."

There was no reasoning with her, and honestly, why should there be? Here I was running off with a bridesmaid on nothing more than a hunch. What if we found out that Ellie and Al were fine, and it made me late for the day I had been waiting for my entire life? What if Ben finally said enough is enough and dumped her for someone who more closely resembled his mother's idea of perfect domesticity?

"I would never break Ben's heart. I love him." I tried to step forward, but she wasn't budging.

"Turn around, young lady," Leslie commanded.

"Stop, Leslie," a voice bellowed from behind us. "Let this poor girl go do what she needs to do." Ben's aunt Joanie stood in an almost identical stance as her sister, arms crossed and chin defiant.

"This is none of your business," Leslie said, dismissing her little sister.

"If it has to do with Ben, it is very much my business." Joanie turned her gaze to me. "You really think your cousin is in danger?"

"I do," I pleaded.

"And you, Officer Oliva, do you agree there's a reason to go check on her?" Joanie asked, using Mary's professional title. I like that she did that.

"Yes, ma'am, I do. Dot here is full of all kinds of crazy theories, until they start to sound quite sane. Trust me, I wouldn't be going with her if I didn't think there was a good chance Ellie was in trouble. With the baby coming so soon, we can't fool around."

"That's good enough for me. Leslie, you need to move."

Leslie lifted her chin. "What about Ben?"

"I'll tell Ben about it. He knows Dot better than we do, and if she says she needs to do this, I'll bet he'll understand. Now move."

"It's just...I don't think..." Leslie stammered.

"Just because I didn't give you that perfect marriage you wanted doesn't mean that Dot and Ben can't have one. You just have to let go a little bit, Les. Can you do that?"

Leslie looked at her feet and then quietly stepped aside. Yes, I needed to get to know Aunt Joanie. She was a keeper.

Ben's car was parked out front, complete with tin cans and a Just Married sign in the back window. Right as we stepped onto the sidewalk, the sky burst out in a downpour, and a lightning bolt lit up the sky, reflecting on the spot poor Earl had landed. I spotted Ben's keys on the dashboard. I jumped in just as the rain started pelting my freshly styled hair. Mary hopped into the passenger seat, making me think of Batman and Robin. Holy Matrimony, Batman.

Chapter Twenty-Five

"Where are we going?" Mary asked. "Where do you think Ellie is? I followed you out here, and now I'm worried you don't actually have a plan."

"I think she's at the house of the church organist."

She cocked her head to the side. "What? Why her?"

"I think she wants Ellie's baby."

"What would bring you to that conclusion? What kind of person would take another woman's baby? Why would you say such a thing?"

"I can't be sure, but she doted on Ellie every time she was near her. After hearing what Clarence just said, I know it sounds crazy. But think about it. She kept talking about other people having babies and even told us she was a nurse. She has the medical training to steal Ellie's baby. I think she feels she needs a baby to keep her boyfriend around. She might be desperate, and, well, don't forget there was a kidnapping attempt of a pregnant woman over in Bexar County. I don't know if all of this is connected, but I can't take a chance that it is."

Mary held her gaze out the window as she thought. "You are crazy. Do you know you just about gave Ben's mother a heart attack back there, not to mention a fight between sisters? I need to look at the facts. First, Al is missing."

"Right. And who is there for Ellie to protect her and take care of her? Al. He had to be eliminated. I just hope that doesn't mean whoever did this threw him off a belfry somewhere."

"Oh my God. Now you're talking about mass murder."

"If Charlotte killed Earl," I said. "She could kill Al."

"OK. Now you're making me start to wish I had a place to hang a gun belt on this dress. Then there's Ellie, who suddenly disappeared. Poof. She's gone. That would mean they would have to be waiting somewhere around the church to get her alone."

"Yes, and with all the people coming and going today, they could go unnoticed."

Mary nodded. "Especially if they told her they knew where Al was. She'd get in their car without a peep. All right, I'm on board. Ellie's in trouble. Do you know where Charlotte lives? That is, if they would be stupid enough to bring her to their house."

"I think I do. She's close by. One time she told me about living above a barber shop."

"Seriously? I didn't know people actually lived in those spaces above the stores," Mary said.

"Me either."

I pulled into a lot at the back of the barber shop and parked Ben's car next to a maroon car. I was sure it was the same car Ellie thought was following her. I knew we were in the right place. The cans on the back of our car were making a racket, but luckily, the rain and thunder helped to hide the noise.

"That's their car."

"How do you know that? Did Charlotte drive it to the church?"

"No. That car has been following Ellie for the last week."

Mary looked surprised. "And you knew this and didn't tell me?"

"We weren't sure, but if it makes you feel better, I was going to tell you, it just slipped my mind."

Mary, who had a few confrontations with wrongdoers, pushed in front of me. "Let me lead. This could get dangerous."

We jumped into the downpour and ran for the stairs that led to the upstairs apartment.

I let her get in front of me, and we started up a set of creaky wooden stairs. I had to hope our footsteps on the battered wood wouldn't warn them of our presence. All our attempts at being stealthy, though, went out the window when we got to the door at the top of the landing that was covered by a small awning, and Mary banged on the door.

"Police. Open the door." I had no idea a woman as small as Mary could make that much noise.

Even though her voice was deafening, there was no sound on the other side. There was an old Chevy in the parking lot, so it either belonged to Charlotte or her boyfriend. If Ellie wasn't in there, I felt a surge of dread. She had to be in there. I stepped in front of Mary and knocked.

"Ellie? Are you in there?" I yelled.

Again, there was no sound, and then something clunked on the other side. It sounded like something heavy had fallen to the floor. It could be Ellie or something she was using to make noise.

I pounded on the door. "Ellie, is that you? It's me, Dot. If that's you, let me know you're okay, okay? I'm not going to leave until I know you are all right."

The door suddenly flew open, and the man Dot had seen on the street with Charlotte filled the doorway. This was Mac. He wore the same outfit I had seen him in the other day, except the leather jacket was gone. He had his fingers in his belt loops, and he snapped gum between words.

"What?" he snapped. "I don't know who this Ellie is, but she's not here. Get lost."

There was more noise in the background, like something hitting the floorboards. "What about Charlotte? Do you know where she is?"

He smirked. "Charlotte who? I don't know a Charlotte. I live here alone." He put a meaty hand on the doorframe, about to close it.

I stuck a white go-go boot in the door and held fast. "I don't think so. I saw you with her just the other day."

His smile grew bigger, stretching to the corners of his mouth as he looked down at my leg exposed in the mini-dress. "Then you're wrong, daisy girl. Scram. I think you need to mind your own business." I had forgotten I was still wearing the daisy crown in my hair. Sadly, I had also forgotten I was about to be late to my own wedding. All I cared about right now was Ellie and the baby. I had to hope Ben would understand.

CHAPTER TWENTY-FIVE

Mac was bigger than me, even with in my high-heeled white plastic boots.

Mary stuck her foot in the door next to mine. "If you really want us to go, then let us come in and look around. What's the harm if you're all that innocent?"

He drew his eyebrows together, the smile suddenly gone, and his tone became menacing. "I don't have to do anything for you."

Even though there were two of us and one of him, we were losing. Maybe he really did live alone, and we were harassing the man, but I was sure I heard noises in the background. Something was going on in that apartment, and I had to know. "I saw you with Charlotte a few days ago near the flower shop. I know you're her boyfriend."

"I don't know who you saw, but it wasn't me. Maybe you should pay a visit to your eye doctor, Daisy."

I was getting desperate. I had to get into that apartment. I tried to slow my breathing. "That's fine. I've already called the police. They'll search the apartment. There are some pretty big guys on the force."

Mary leaned forward. "Really big. Bigger than you."

The noise in the background ramped up, and I leaned on the door. Mac stepped closer, gum snapping, and towered over both of us. "How did you call the cops? A magic phone in your pocket?"

"Actually, I'm a cop. I know I don't look like it in this dress, but you see, we're about to be in a wedding." Mary kept rambling, but then, to my surprise, she tried to muscle past the big guy. He stopped her with a shove, knocking her down the rickety steps, but in the process, I slid by and ran into the apartment. I had to hope Mary was unharmed and that she hadn't fallen all the way down the steps. If she was lying at the bottom on the ground, I would never forgive myself. Once inside, I knew my instinct had been correct.

Chapter Twenty-Six

The first thing to hit my sightline was Al. He was still dressed in blue jeans and blue chambray shirt with his name stitched above the pocket. It was the outfit I had seen on him at the Uphill Bar before the bachelor party. Al struggled against a hemp rope looped tightly around him. He tried to speak around a dirty gag in his mouth that looked like an old t-shirt. Across from Al was the leather jacket I had seen Mac wearing that day on the street. Suddenly, a sharp crack of thunder split the air, making a bare bulb hanging above Al swing. A rusty oscillating fan whirred on a stained kitchen counter, causing one of the daisies, so carefully placed in my hair, to fall to the filthy wood floor. The rain outside was light at first, but then increased gradually. A smell of stale beer emanated through the room, and a sourness mixed with the tang of ozone carried by the storm. Al was stuck, but his eyes were dancing, motioning me to a closed door. Looking around for a weapon, I found a broken curtain rod on the floor next to the window. Grabbing it, I pulled open the door, hearing Mac's footsteps behind me.

I found Ellie in a back bedroom, lying on a sagging bed of disheveled sheets. Her wrist was fastened to the bedpost, and a scarf, wound tightly around her jaw, served as a gag, preventing her from calling for help. She was wearing the blue silk bridesmaid dress she had so carefully constructed for my wedding, an event that seemed miles away at this point. Standing over her was Charlotte, holding a small knife I recognized as a scalpel. A bolt of lightning struck outside, making Charlotte look like a mad scientist out of a Saturday afternoon matinee at the Rialto. She wore a white floral dress that flowed with the movement of the oscillating fan. Her eyes were wild and focused on Ellie's unborn baby.

"What are you doing? Get away from her!" I screamed, dropped the curtain rod, and leaped forward, intending to pull the scalpel out of her hand. If it cut me, fine, but at least it wouldn't be slicing into Ellie.

From behind me, I felt powerful arms squeezing my biceps, pulling me away like a child from a doll. I struggled against Mac, knocking us both into a table where Charlotte had set up a station with a bowl of hot water and antiseptic. Both fluids spilled over us both, but then Mac pulled me up from the floor. I squirmed against him, but his grip was too strong.

"Charlotte, you can't do this," I screamed. "Let her go!"

Charlotte had always seemed like a sane person whenever I talked to her, but now I could see she was driven. Driven for what she thought would be a happy ending. How could she think it was right for her future husband to demand a baby she couldn't produce, except through violence against another?

"Don't worry," she said, her tone placating and a direct contrast to my screams. "Remember? I told you I was a nurse. I know what I'm doing. This is our baby I'm saving."

Aunt Mavis was a nurse, and she would never do something like this. The room was dirty and unkempt. "If you are going to use that scalpel, any good nurse would know you should have sedated Ellie. What you are about to do is torture."

"Shut up," Charlotte snapped, her calming tone gone in an instant. "I have to do this." It seemed so plain when she said it that way. She was sure what she was doing was perfectly acceptable. "Your cousin is simply the cocoon. She means nothing. She's just another pregnant woman in North Texas. Besides, she can have more babies. I can't. We've waited too long not to take what is rightfully ours."

Ellie's muffled scream came through the gag as she tried to pull from her wrist restraint. I was shocked by how cold Charlotte was. "What do you mean? You intend to cut open an innocent woman and steal her baby?" I asked.

Mac leaned over me. "This is our baby. But we're not going to be calling him Al. What a lousy name. Nope. This kid is going to be called Steve. You know, like Steve McQueen. A really cool character who won't put up with any—"

"Is that why you killed Earl?" I interrupted. "He told me he had a way of hearing about everything in the church. Did he overhear you two planning to steal someone's baby? I'll also bet that Ellie isn't your first attempt. You were the ones who tried to grab a woman in Bexar County. Earl found out, didn't he? You two were talking in the sanctuary, and he heard something."

Charlotte scowled. "That old busybody. And for your information, you're all wrong. I would never do anything as stupid as plan to commit a crime and discuss it out loud at the church."

"No? Then what?" As I spoke, Ellie nodded, and I heard noise in the next room.

Charlotte raised her chin, her upflip hitting the back of her neck. "I don't profess to be a perfect Christian, but I did want to tell God what I was trying to do and why I was doing it. I figured if I cleared the air before I did it, then all would be fine. I think God wanted me to be happy and raise a child for him. If I can't have a baby, I decided I would help someone raise their baby. It was a noble thing to do, so I was sitting in the pews talking to that big wooden cross up front. I was dedicating myself to the life of this child, and I began crying in the chapel."

"And Earl overheard you?"

"Yes. It was that damn leak. A real handyman would have found it, but he was always crawling around in the attic looking for it and overheard me through the vent."

"And he confronted you?"

Charlotte nodded her head. "Oh yes. He said God would never want me to do what I was doing. Why would he think it was his business to tell me what to do? He threatened me. He told me he was going to go to the police, but if I canceled my plan, he'd leave it alone. It was the forgiving thing to do. That's the problem with Camden Chapel. People think they have the right to get into your business."

"Even so, how can you be sure he wouldn't go to the police? What he overheard was kidnapping and a possibility of attempted murder if the mother dies. It wasn't like you were confessing you wanted to tell off Vernice."

"He was an idiot, a gullible one at that. I lied and told him I respected what he had to say. Because of him, I changed my mind and promised I would never do anything like that. I was having a moment of temporary insanity, and then he hugged me. Church people," she said in disgust.

"That was it? That was all you had to do?"

"Come on. The guy spent his days changing light bulbs. He was easy to fool."

"Did you know he used to be a cop?"

Mac laughed. "You're putting us on. Earl was a cop? If he was, he wasn't a very good one."

"Killing him was easy," Charlotte said. "I brought him a muffin when he was working at the church. The old guy had a sweet tooth. He gobbled it down and even told me how good it tasted right before he hit the floor of the sanctuary. Then Mac and I took him up to the belfry. Once up there, I went back down and started playing the organ. Mac waited a few minutes and then threw him over. After that, he slipped out the side door."

Ellie continued to twist around on the bed, trying to free herself.

"So, when I found him, you had an alibi. We could all hear you playing the organ."

"Yeah. I'm not stupid. I was still hyped up when I came outside, but everyone thought it was because poor Earl the busboy went splat. Nope. It was because I had just gotten away with murder."

I remembered her hands shaking as she smoked a cigarette on the church lawn. I checked on Ellie, looking into her eyes. She was terrified, and her skin was bright red. I had to keep stalling and figure out how to free her, even though I was being held by Mac.

"What about Vernice?" I asked.

"Vernice." She said the name like it left a bad taste in her mouth. "That woman. I have to say, killing her was my pleasure. I had to do it after she found that piece of paper. The minute she centered on something, she was like a dog with a bone. She thought she was doing us all a favor by returning someone's scribbling back to the rightful owner. She had it in her mind some poor sap had been sitting in church writing down their work schedule. It's amazing the stories she could make up in her mind about people."

"But that wasn't what it was?"

"It was a list of Ellie's movements during the day. I'm surprised she didn't recognize my handwriting. I wrote it. I made it for Mac so he could follow her. He does better at things when you write it down. He came by the sanctuary, and I gave it to him, but then we got distracted, and he left it in the pew. Idiot."

Ellie let out a whine on the bed, and when I glanced over, her knees were bent, with her hands gripping the sheet. I had to keep talking and searched for the last thing Charlotte had said.

"Got distracted?"

Charlotte shook her head. "Not that it's any of your business, but no one was in the church, and we…uh…we…" She blushed. "They need to pad those pews. Anyway, I brought her some carrot cake because it was pretty obvious she couldn't say no to anything sweet. I used to watch her fill up her plate at all those potlucks. I think she was eating away her feelings because her husband was always gone. We put sedatives in Earl's cupcake, and it worked so well, we put rat poison in her carrot cake."

"So, you poisoned both of them with baked goods?"

"What can I say? I have a gift. Maybe I should open a bakery." She turned her focus back to Ellie, who was squirming on the bed. "Now I'm taking what's rightfully mine."

"No, wait," I begged. I had to stop her. I had to play for time.

Ellie screamed as Charlotte drew near, but then there was a clatter in the other room, and I had to hope Al had found a way to free himself. The rain picked up outside as we experienced the kind of late summer Texas storm that rivaled a hurricane. The sound of the rain was so loud, Charlotte yelled. "You can't stop me. Mac, take her out of here." There was more noise in the next room. Ellie let out a scream from beneath the gag. Her eyes widened, and she tried to scoot herself up to the headboard.

I stomped on Mac's foot, and he bellowed, letting go of his grip for a second. I tried to struggle free, but he pulled me back. I screamed over the rain. "No, it's Ellie and Al's baby. You have nothing to do with that child. He's not yours. Step away from her." Ellie's cheeks were bright red now, and she looked in pain. She grimaced and let out a sound I had never heard come from her. Even though it was foreign to me, I knew what it was. It wasn't because Charlotte was towering over her with a scalpel. She was having the baby.

Charlotte leaned closer and raised the scalpel. I screamed over the deafening rain. "Wait! You don't have to cut her. I think the baby is coming on its own. Just wait, please."

Charlotte looked sideways at me from her bent-over position. For the first time, her confidence looked a little shaky. "How do you know?"

Ellie vigorously nodded up and down and started trying to talk from behind the scarf.

"She's trying to tell you. The baby is coming. She's in labor." I struggled against Mac's grasp. I had to help Ellie. "Where is Mary? What did you do to her?"

"Don't worry about her. She's at the bottom of the stairs. By the time they find her, we'll be gone." Mac snarled.

I pictured Mary unconscious on the ground, the rain pelting her. I didn't know if she was alive or dead, but if she had become their third victim, anger filled me. "You'll never get away with this," I threatened. "You have no right to this baby. I will make sure that you pay for everything you've done. Your insanity has led to the deaths of two people, and now you're adding to the score."

"Sure, we will," Charlotte boasted. "We'll get our baby, and split town. No one will ever see us again. We have it all worked out." Ellie began screaming behind the gag as Charlotte drew closer, the scalpel glimmering in a ray of sun from the window.

The more Ellie screamed, the more I pushed forward. "The police will find you. I'll guarantee it. If you hurt Mary, then it's a whole different thing. Cops go crazy when one of their own is hurt. You've crossed a line, and you can't go back. They'll put on extra patrols, and they'll make sure that wherever you go, they find you. Pushing a cop down the stairs was a really stupid idea, but then again, you two aren't the sharpest knives in the drawer, now are you? I'll tell them everything you just told me."

The grip tightened around my arm. "You aren't going to be talking to anyone. Too bad how you died on your wedding day. So sad," she said the last part in baby talk, making my stomach fill with rage. The thoughts of my wedding day, Ben waiting at the altar, Ben's mother, and my mother went way back in my psyche. All I could think of was here and now and how I was going to stop this woman or die trying.

Chapter Twenty-Seven

What had happened to Al in the next room? I couldn't hear any more noises as the rain pounded on the roof. Even if he broke through, there was no way he could be of any help. Ellie let out a scream and started clenching the sheets again.

"It's happening. She's having the baby!" I screamed, pulling so hard, both Mac and I moved closer. Ellie cried out again.

Mac shot a look at Ellie. "Take a look at her, honey. See if there's a baby coming out."

Charlotte seemed puzzled and slightly nervous. "I...I don't know."

Ellie was screaming again. I squirmed, trying to get away from Mac. "You said you were a nurse. Take a look at her," I shouted.

Charlotte's grip on the scalpel tightened, her hands shaking. "I wasn't in labor and delivery. I took care of old people."

"So, you don't know anything about babies, and you were about to do a C-section on my cousin, and you had no idea what you were doing? You were going to kill my cousin and let her bleed out on the bed? What kind of monster are you?" I wrenched one arm free and then the other, which might have seemed like a Herculean feat, but I realized Mac had let go. When I glanced at him, he looked shocked that his girlfriend was about to cut someone open with no knowledge of what she was doing.

"I thought she'd be asleep," he said.

I ran to Ellie, making my way around Charlotte and her scalpel. Charlotte started to move forward, but I pushed her so hard she hit the floor, the scalpel clanging across the wood boards, landing near the doorway. I also didn't know anything about delivering babies, but I had no choice. I quickly checked under the skirt of her blue bridesmaid dress. It didn't take long for me to figure out that she and the bed were soaked with clear fluid. I began to remove her underthings, and when I did, I jumped back. It was like something out of a horror movie. I saw a tiny head, just an inch out. Al, Jr. was on his way out into the world. "The baby's head is, uh, sticking out."

Charlotte positioned herself behind me and yelled, quite unnecessarily. "Get it out. Get our baby out."

I didn't know what to do, but I put on my best Dr. Kildare and tried to look like I did. I also realized I was the one in control right now. Charlotte just wanted that baby, so anything I did, she would think was necessary for the delivery. I reached up and untied the scarf around Ellie's mouth and then the ties at her arms.

"Don't untie her," Charlotte shouted. "She'll get away and take our baby. Tie her back up!"

"I have to untie her if we are going to do this. The restraints are putting stress on the baby. Ellie needs to feel secure, or it could prolong her labor. You understand that, don't you?" I was making the whole thing up, but Charlotte seemed to be buying it because she began to nod.

Ellie, her mouth now free, let out a giant keening, and as she did, the baby came farther out. If she kept this up, we would have a baby in no time. The only problem was, I wasn't a doctor. If something unexpected happened, I wouldn't know what to do. I had to hope and pray there would be no complications. Al, Jr. had to be safe with me delivering him. Ellie went into another contraction, and as she did, I heard a scuffle from behind us. Al's voice towered above it all.

"Out of my way. My wife's having our baby." Al held the scalpel in his hand and gestured in a slashing movement toward Mac. I had no doubt that if Mac tried to take a step forward, Al would slice him badly.

Mac stepped back. "How did you get free? I tied those knots well."

"I had help. Mary's on her way with the police. Give it up. I'm getting my wife to the hospital. We are not having our baby in this place."

Charlotte, the light of the storm behind her white dress, screamed, her eyes wild, her hair picked up by the breeze from the fan. "It's our baby, not yours."

"I'm going to make sure you go to prison for the rest of your life," Al said.

Charlotte looked from Al to me and then finally to Ellie on the bed. "We need to get out of here, Mac. Right now."

"But our baby—"

"Shut up!"

She started for the door. "Just remember, no matter what happens. You're raising *our* baby, and someday, we'll be back for him."

"Over my dead body," Al said.

Charlotte screamed again. "I'll do it. Don't think I won't."

She ran out the door with Mac lumbering after her.

Al turned back to me as the sound of a car starting filled the air of the apartment. Charlotte and Mac were getting away. "Thank God for you, Dot. She would have killed her."

Ellie screamed and pushed. The baby was farther out, but still, only part of the head was visible. "It's okay, Ellie. You're safe now. Let's have this baby."

There was the sound of heavy footsteps in the next room, but my focus was on the baby. Ellie began to scream, and Al went into coach mode. "That's it. Push that baby out. I want to see his whole head this time." As she pushed, there was a tap on my shoulder. An ambulance crew had appeared behind me. Ben rushed in behind them with Dusty bringing up the rear. Eyeing what was going on, Dusty made a face and turned the other way.

Ben was at my elbow. "I found you. You didn't run out on me on our wedding day." He looked down at Ellie. "Oh my God. Is she?"

"Yes."

He wrinkled his nose up. "Is that the baby sticking out?"

The paramedic had now taken my place at Ellie's bedside.

"So, she's having the baby now? Here?"

"Looks like it."

I felt an overwhelming sense of relief as I watched the professionals take over. Ellie was going to be all right, and Al Jr., no matter what happened, would be in the hands of doctors, not people like me or Charlotte.

"What's all over the bed?" Al said, pointing to the stained sheets.

The paramedic reassured Al. "Don't worry. That was the amniotic fluid. Your wife's water broke. It's absolutely normal, so stay calm. We will get her to the hospital just as soon as she delivers. Right now, we just need to be calm."

"Be calm," Al started repeating as he began to pace the floorboards of the dilapidated room. "I can't believe my kid's birthplace is going to be above a barber shop."

"I should have known, Dot Morgan," Ben said. "Aunt Joanie told me you left, but I didn't know where to find you until the police drove by the church. I had no idea where they were going, but Dusty said maybe they'd found Al and Ellie, so we hopped in my parents' car and followed them. I was surprised when they stopped at a barber shop. Something like this always happens. Are you okay?"

"I'm fine." I went into Ben's arms, feeling the warmth and comfort I needed in this moment. My eyes met Dusty's. If it weren't for him, Ben would still be waiting at the church. "Thank you, Dusty." The big man looked embarrassed but finally acknowledged me with a small nod.

"I'm so sorry I ran out on our wedding day," I said to Ben.

"I'll forgive you this time," he whispered into my ear.

"Okay, ma'am. The baby is almost out. One more big push," the paramedic gently coached.

"You can do it, Ellie," Al cheered from behind him. "I can see our baby. He's beautiful."

Dusty put a hand up. "Could we continue this in the next room? Give the lady some privacy."

"Oh, yeah. Sorry about that." Ben and I joined Dusty in the room where Al had been held captive. The chair was on its side, the ropes strewn across the floor. The rain, I noticed, had let up, and if it continued that way, I might actually have a blue sky on my wedding day.

Once out of the room where the delivery was going on, Dusty let out a breath. "Man, Ben. You were right all along. Dot here is a murder magnet."

Ben hugged me hard. "I know, I know. I would add to that, she's the queen of unpredictable. I just never know from one day to the next."

He was right. I ran away on my wedding day, and even though his mother demanded I stay, I left him at the altar. I'd put him through more than one moment of fear for my safety. "And you still want to marry me?"

"Frankly," Dusty said to Ben. "I'd be thinking real hard right now."

"I stopped thinking the first time she smiled at me. I'm in it for the long haul." Ben answered, his lips in my hair.

Five minutes later, my second cousin, a beautiful little girl—yes, a girl named Alice—was officially a part of our lives. They decided to drop the idea of making her a junior.

Chapter Twenty-Eight

"So, are we still getting married today?" Ben asked as the paramedics took Ellie and little Alice away in the ambulance.

"What time is it?" I asked.

"2:30. The wedding was supposed to start a half hour ago," Dusty said, holding up his watch.

"Do you think anyone is still there? Would they have made an announcement and sent everyone home?"

Ben shrugged. "If I know my mother and how much she wants me to marry you, I would say she's probably barring the door right now."

"So are we going back for her or for us? Sometimes I wonder about how much you try to please your mother."

"Maybe you're right. I do try too hard. I just see that look she gets when she's disappointed in me."

"How many times have you seen that?" I asked.

"Enough to know I don't like it."

"What about me? What if you disappoint me?"

"I…uh…see what you mean. You're right. All through the lead-up to the wedding, I've tried to keep everybody happy, especially my mother. Now I'm beginning to realize maybe that can't be done. Somebody, sometime will be disappointed, right?"

"I'm afraid so. You don't have to please everybody all the time, Ben."

"I don't, do I?"

"Nope. Your mom will recover, whatever you do. That's because she loves you, pretty unconditionally. You just haven't always seen it. Okay, let's go and check out what's happening at the church. After all this, I kind of feel like the whole wedding thing…"

"There's that word," Ben cautioned.

"Sorry. I feel like all the worry we had about the wedding"—I paused so he could hear I wasn't calling it a thing—"Is nothing compared to what I just went through. I also feel like I want to marry you more than ever. The most important thing about weddings is not the cake or the flowers or the dresses. It's the promise. The promise that you will be there for me and I will be there for you, no matter what."

Dusty quickly agreed. "Right. No matter how many homicidal murderers you meet, you at least have each other."

When we returned to the church, the guests were, unbelievably, sitting in the pews waiting for a wedding. Most of them, anyway. Ben ran to the front, and the chattering among the remaining crowd ceased. Pastor Ross and Davita rose from the front pew, and Clarence stood while, at the same time, he hushed his chattering choir by raising his hand. "Looks like there might be a wedding after all, everybody. Thank you for your patience. Stay tuned."

Clarence then stepped forward from the assembled choir. "I know this is rather impromptu, but the choir has been practicing several songs, and we'd love to try them out on you. Davita? Would you join us?"

Davita made her way past the pastor. "I'd love to, Clarence."

Pastor Ross moved to the front of the church, his hands together. "Wonderful. Let's all have a moment of prayer while we await the bride."

As the choir started filling the sanctuary with music, my mother, Aunt Mavis, Ben's mother, and Joanie followed us back to the Sunday school room where we had dressed earlier. Once inside the room, I grabbed Aunt Mavis's arm. "I need you to know that Ellie is okay. She had the baby."

Aunt Mavis gasped in a breath so hard I worried she would hurt herself. "She what? She went to the hospital, and you didn't tell me? That's why she ran out of here? I can't believe she would just go into labor and not tell anyone. I could have been there. I could have helped her."

"I wish you had been," I said, thinking my aunt's job was pretty amazing.

"It wasn't quite like that. She was kidnapped."

The confusion spread over her features. "She was *what*? Are you serious? Someone kidnapped my Ellie? Somehow that's supposed to make it better? What are you saying?"

"I know it sounds crazy, but both she and Al were being held captive over the barber shop."

"The barber kidnapped them? I've known Lawrence for years. Why would he do such a thing?"

"No. The barber shop wasn't open because Lawrence is here at the wedding. It was Charlotte. She wanted Ellie's baby."

With that, Joanie fell into the first chair she could find. "Damn. I know you brag about this little town, Leslie, but I had no idea it was this exciting. You've been holding back."

"What is all over your dress?" My mother asked. I looked down at the beautiful dress Ellie had made for me. It was worthy of *Bride's* magazine, and now it was ruined. It was dirty and stained from when the hot water and antiseptic fell on me during my struggle with Mac.

Mavis reached for her bag. "I need to get Howard. We have to go. We have to be there at the delivery."

"Wait. Aunt Mavis, she's already had the baby. She's fine, and her little girl is beautiful. Al is over the moon—"

"Al, Jr., is a girl?" Mavis's face lit up, and she slapped her knees. "It's a girl! Another strong woman in the Monroe family. I have to get Howard. Is she at the hospital?"

"Yes."

"I'm sorry, Dot, but I'm going to miss your wedding. I have to meet my new granddaughter." She turned to my mother. "Sorry, Opal. I need to leave your daughter to get to mine." They hugged.

"You go, Mavis. Congratulations," my mother said.

Leslie, who had been quiet through all of this, had a strange look on her face. Then, to my surprise, she reached out and hugged me. She whispered in my ear. "Thank goodness you're unharmed. We were so worried."

I hugged her back. It was the sweetest thing she had ever said to me.

"I think I have a solution for the dress. Give me five minutes." My mother ran out of the room. I had no idea what kind of soap she planned to use, but the dress was pretty well totaled.

"Can I come in?" Mary stood in the doorway, a Band-Aid on her head and her arm in a sling. I had never been so glad to see her.

"What happened to you? Are you alright? I can't believe you're actually here." The words rushed from my mouth.

"Yes, I'm here. I was injured, so the police department sent me home, and well, there was this wedding, and I heard there might be an opening for a matron of honor, that is, if you'll have me by your side."

For the first time, I started to cry. "I would be honored for you to be my matron of honor."

Mary's eyes rimmed with moisture. "After everything that has happened, I have this insane motivation to not let you out of my sight."

"Can you tell us? Did they catch Charlotte and Mac?" I asked. If they were successful in getting away after two murders and a double, no triple kidnapping, they would surely hit the most wanted list. It also meant that they could be out there waiting for the right moment to grab the baby they felt was theirs.

"We caught them at the gas station. I guess when planning their getaway, Mac forgot to do one of his jobs. Filling his car with gas. They were driving a maroon Chevy sedan."

"The same maroon car that had been following Ellie."

Mary looked surprised. "Yes, the car you noticed following her around and didn't tell me about. When they surrounded them, we thought that hulk, Mac, would put up a fight, but he went peacefully. It seems he's not so brave when he has to go against men his size. We have both of them down at the station. She's started bragging about killing Earl and Vernice. She's just a little on the nutty side. I was going to stay, but Barrerra sent me home, which was fine because there was no way I was going to miss you going down the aisle."

"I'm somewhere between shaking and exhausted. I can't believe they are in custody. She was going to kill Ellie," I said.

"Yes. Doing a C-section like that would have caused so much blood loss, Ellie would have died."

"And it all started with this caretaker? Talk about being in the wrong place at the wrong time. Poor guy," Aunt Joanie said.

"Earl knew too much. She drugged him, and Mac threw him off the belfry. When they killed Vernice, Charlotte skipped sedation and went straight to poison. The way she was talking, it was nothing to her."

"I'm just glad Ellie is okay," Joanie said. "I'm going to need a vacation after this wedding."

Leslie then took my arm and said, "She is okay, and you are too. So, I need to ask. Are you ready to marry my son now?"

My head was spinning. Somehow, I had just returned to the way I was feeling in the morning when I woke up, but this time, I was sure. "Yes. More than ever."

I glanced at Joanie, Leslie's sister, then back to my future mother-in-law. "I'm not sure I'm exactly the person you want me to be. I was trying really hard to be the perfect daughter-in-law, but now you know. Things like this happen to me. I admire everything you do. Your home, your incredible dinners, and your love of your family—I don't think I could ever be as good as you are at that kind of thing. Ben was lucky to be raised by you, but I was raised by a working mother. I learned early on to help with dinner and the housework. I loved hearing about her tales of the library, and I never thought there was anything wrong with it. My mom is one of my heroes."

"I see that now," Leslie said. "I also think I'm seeing you, the real you, for the first time." She let out a tiny laugh. "Ben is going to have his hands full. We all are, but I think you are a splendid addition to our family, and eventually I think you'll have a house full of children."

I loved what she was saying, but noted the grandchild suggestion was still neatly fitted into our conversation.

"I'm back." My mother stood at the door holding a zipped-up garment bag. "I'm not sure if this will fit, but this is the dress I wore when I married your dad. I think I was about the same size you are now."

I put a hand over my mouth. My mother was a genius. She unzipped the garment bag, and there it was. It was a stunning liquid satin gown with beaded appliques at the sweetheart neckline and waist. There was defined seamed detailing and shoulder pads. It was a gem from the forties, and even though the hem fell gracefully, it was detailed with satin rosettes and pearls. My mini-skirt was the fashion of the day, but so was this beautiful dress.

"Can I wear it?" I asked.

"Please wear it. I loved your dress, but I also would love to see my daughter in my wedding dress," she said.

Leslie then guided me to the changing room divider. "Try it on. I can't wait to see it."

Twenty minutes later, I walked down the aisle, wearing my mother's wedding dress and holding a bouquet of white daisies. Instead of organ music, the choir had taken over with an a cappella version of the wedding march.

Ben caught sight of me and gasped, then a smile spread across his face. Dusty elbowed him and gave me a wink. He was taller than Ben, and I would bet he was taller than anyone in the church. Still, his presence was welcome here.

As I walked down the aisle, I looked into the eyes of the people I loved. Arlene sat on the end of one pew, tissue in hand. On the other side was Joe Columbo from the best Italian restaurant in North Texas. The librarians all sat in one row, tittering little whispers about the dress, as others cleaned their glasses to see it better. Oliver and Dana had made it—employers from my last job, and the barber whose upstairs apartment we had just rescued Ellie from sat proudly with his five children and wife in ignorant bliss of what had just happened.

As I drew closer to Ben, walking through our family and friends, I knew this was a moment I would always cherish. It had been hard to come by, but here it was, and just like my dream, everything was perfect.

Chapter Twenty-Nine

An hour later, we were settled in the church basement for wedding cake and the beautiful meal Vernice had arranged before her death. She would have been so proud of her work. Folding tables were adorned with white tablecloths, and a bouquet of white daisies, mixed in with greenery and a tiny ceramic bee, was placed on the head table for Ben and me and our parents. White balloons bobbed near the ceiling with a handmade poster stating "Just Married" in case anyone wasn't aware of that fact. One corner of the room had been designated as a makeshift buffet with serving dishes of roast chicken, creamy mashed potatoes, yeast rolls, and green beans. I noticed there were a few dishes that were not on Vernice's menu and suspected some of the ladies brought fruit salads and molded Jell-O to add to the occasion. At the end of the table was our wedding cake, a simple two-cake setup with a tiny blond bride and brunette groom on the top, smiling out at the crowd in all of their glorified plastic. After all we'd been through, it was a wonder the cake maker didn't put a little yellow garland of crime scene tape as part of the garnish.

My heart warmed to the sounds of polite chatter and silverware clinking on the church's dinnerware. Two little boys were running around the tables wreaking havoc, and I noticed Davita Ross settling them down and ushering them back to Eddie. I had never met Vernice's boys, but I knew this must be them. They were a lot to handle, and I wasn't sure Eddie was the man to do it. This was my first time seeing him as well, and although he did bear a striking resemblance to Tony Curtis, he looked like he had been working a double shift, and truthfully, being a parent of those two would feel like it.

Sitting next to him sat our florist, Lily.

"Why is Lily sitting next to Eddie Schaeffer?" I whispered in Ben's ear. "I didn't think she knew Vernice."

Ben looked over. "I have no idea. There aren't that many tables here. Maybe she went for an unoccupied seat and happened to be next to him. It's too bad she has to sit there with those little boys. They're tearing this place up."

"Give them a break. They just lost their mother. I'm surprised Eddie is even here."

"He probably brought them because they are getting a free meal." Lily's eyes were red, and Eddie placed his hand over hers.

He put a hand to his chin. "You're right. She looks like she chose to be there." Someone was waving at Ben. "I'll be right back." Ben kissed me and went to the table that beckoned him.

Davita sat both boys down at the table with Eddie and Lily and tried to keep them occupied.

"Doesn't she do well with children?" Pastor Ross said over my shoulder. "I always wanted kids, but Davita, well, she has other things she wants to pursue."

"I'm so glad she sang for us today. Your wife has a beautiful voice," I said. I remembered the conversation I had with Davita a few days earlier. Did the pastor know about the hidden suitcase?

He looked down at his hands. "Thank you. I'll be sure to tell her. You see, my wife is a singer. That was her passion before she met me, and it still is. I'm afraid I tried to put her into a box she didn't deserve to be in. Selfish, I know."

I did know. I was fighting out of my own box. "But now?" I asked.

"Now, we've talked about it, and I think we have something that might work. She's going to start singing again."

"That's wonderful. Back in Dallas?"

"Yes, but our choir director, Clarence, has graciously offered to let her sing with his—what did he call it, combo? They came to me yesterday with the plan. At first, I thought it wasn't a good idea, but then the more I thought about how she would be with Clarence, I felt better. He's a good man, and I know he won't let anything bad happen to her in the sinful streets of Dallas."

I laughed. "I never heard it described that way, but that's so good to hear. She told me about wanting to sing after I told her my in-laws"—I lowered my voice because Leslie and Clark were only a few feet away—"wanted me to give up working. I don't have a glamorous job like Davita; I just work as a secretary, and well, there have been some…incidents."

"I read the paper. You can call them murders," the pastor said flatly. "I know the Daltons want you two to join the church, but if you don't mind, let me check our insurance policy first."

I laughed.

"You just got married, and it's a blessed event, but that doesn't mean you have to become another person," he said.

"Thank you for saying that, Pastor. I still want to have the freedom, you know?"

"I think I do now. I say you should stand your ground, Mrs. Dalton. The change I've seen in Davita since we've made this decision has been amazing. She's genuinely happy. Something I hadn't seen since we first met. It was the whole reason I fell in love with her in the first place."

"So, I have your blessing?"

"Not that it matters, but of course you do."

Ben, who had been across the room talking to his editor from the *Camden Chronicle*, joined us, slipping his hand around my waist. "Thank you, Pastor Ross, for sticking with us today. There was a while there when I wasn't sure we were having a wedding."

Roger Ross smiled. "I never doubted it for a minute. You two are much too much in love." He gave a little bow and joined Davita, who was now sitting at a table with Clarence, writing something on a napkin. If I had to guess, it was either a song list or a plan of upcoming club dates. Davita was smiling, and Clarence beamed with happiness.

I glanced back over at Lily. "Have you talked to Lily yet?"

"No, but she looks busy."

"I think she's been crying."

"Oh no. I can't believe it's because I got married. She and I are only friends now, or at least I thought so."

"No, it's not that. I didn't tell you this, but when I visited her in her shop, she told me she had bad luck with men." I nodded toward the table. "Now I think it has to do with who she's sitting with."

Ben looked over. "Eddie Schaeffer? I'm afraid I'm not following your thoughts. I saw him pat her hand, but I assumed it's because she's crying."

For an investigative reporter, sometimes Ben was as thick as mud. "Charlotte kept telling me that Vernice's husband, although she told the world he was perfect, was having an affair. I think the other woman might have been Lily."

Ben's eyes widened. "Lily? My Lily? No."

"Look at her. She's been crying, and he's not acting like a grieving husband. All the trips he made to Dallas for business. No one could figure out how he was selling so much there when the real reason was Lily's flower shop was in Dallas. I would bet he was visiting her and telling Vernice he was working."

Ben looked sad. "And then she moved here. Was she thinking that he was going to divorce Vernice?"

"Maybe. If I'm right, who's to say he wasn't stringing her along, making promises? He's already lying to his wife, so why not lie to his mistress?"

Ben looked soulfully at his former girlfriend. At one time in his life, he thought he was going to marry her, but she dumped him right before the wedding. Now I could see his heart was breaking once again. "Poor Lily," he said. "Maybe I should go talk to her."

"I don't know if that's such a good idea. Maybe she doesn't want to talk to you. She might be feeling ashamed or like a foolish woman falling for this guy. What would you say to her? 'Hey, I noticed your affair with a married man isn't going so well?'"

"You're right. Let me think about this. No matter what has happened, the last thing I want to do is make her feel worse," Ben said.

Clarence and his combo were setting up in the corner, the sound of tuning sending discordant notes through the air. Davita left where she was sitting with her husband, her face gleaming with excitement, her cheeks red. She carried a black folder, and when she joined the band, put it on a stand in front of her. She had added a barrette to her hair that sparkled in the overhead lights. Clarence nodded and smiled, and she nodded back. The combo gave a few starting notes, and Davita began to sing a sultry version of *Night and Day*.

"Who is that?" Dusty said, his half-eaten plate of chicken in his large hand.

"That's our pastor's wife, Davita. She's going to sing with the band," Ben said.

"Not her." He pointed to the table where Lily was sitting. "That woman over there. I think she's crying. Is that her husband?"

"Actually," I said, butting into their conversation. "No, but that's another story. She's single."

Dusty's eyebrows raised half an inch. "Really? How single?"

"A little more single than she was last week," Ben said, sighing as he watched her.

Dusty set his plate on the table and then put a fist to his mouth; leaning over to Ben, he said, "Do you think she would like to dance?"

Ben looked at her. "Maybe. But I'd wait until the band starts playing."

"Do you think I can impress her? You know, I worked on the team that opened the Astrodome. You know the spacesuits on the ground crew were my idea."

I acted like he hadn't told me that fact at least once before. Everyone needed a claim to fame, and this was Dusty's. "I think she'll be very impressed," I answered.

That was all it took. Dusty started toward her and then turned back. "Uh, would you introduce us? She might be more willing to dance with me if she knew I was a friend of the groom."

We followed Dusty over, and Ben took the lead. As we approached the table, Eddie, who was still holding her hand, said, "You can't mean that, Lily. It's just that things are different now. I have to think of the boys first. There's no one to take care of them. I just need—"

"Excuse me," Ben said. Lily pulled her hand away from Eddie. "I don't mean to interrupt, but I wanted to introduce Lily to my friend Dusty here.

CHAPTER TWENTY-NINE

We were college roommates, and he wanted to meet you."

"We were talking here, so if you don't mind," Eddie snapped, turning his back on Ben and Dusty.

Lily stood up and dabbed at her eyes with a handkerchief edged in purple flowers. She walked around Eddie and extended her hand. "I'd love to meet your friend, Ben."

Dusty stepped forward. He was clearly almost a foot taller than her, but he bent over and took the same hand Eddie had been holding a moment ago. "Hi. I'm Dusty. If you promise not to believe all the stories Ben tells you about me, would you consider taking a stroll on the dance floor?"

Lily blushed, and her bottom lip trembled. Eddie tried to grab her other hand, but she pulled it away from him. At that moment, the music changed songs, and Davita started singing *True Love*. It was beautiful. Lily smiled up at Dusty. "You know, weddings are wonderful things. They give people new beginnings, don't you think? I'd love to dance."

"Lily—" Eddie's tone bordered on anger. Here was a guy who had hurt two women but then seemed to expect the one he had left to do what he wanted. His arrogance was staggering. Everything Vernice had said about him was wrong. Dead wrong. Charlotte had been right. He was a cheating husband and a jerk.

Lily turned back and smiled. "You need to take care of your boys. I think one of them just smeared a piece of wedding cake on the wall over there."

Eddie's neck turned with a whiplash, and he yelled across the room. "Elroy! You stop that right now. That's it. We're going home." The boy just laughed and ran up the basement stairs. Eddie turned back to us. "Excuse me. This isn't over, Lily."

"Oh, but I think it is." She took Dusty's hand, and he led her out to the makeshift dance floor.

We watched them dance, talking all the while. I was sure he was getting to the spacesuits.

Ben put a hand on his chin. "Hmmm, I never thought of Lily going for a guy like Dusty. You know, it just might work."

"Give them time, Ben. It's just one dance."

"Speaking of which, Mrs. Dalton. Would you like to dance?"

"I would!"

We entered the dance floor, and Clarence quickly shifted gears to the anniversary song. Ben pulled me close as others cleared the floor. I whispered in his ear, "I love you, Ben Dalton. Thank you for marrying me."

He whispered back, "And thank you for working me in to your busy day, Dot Dalton."

"It was the least I could do," I said into his shoulder.

Chapter Thirty

The next day, we were on our way down to South Padre Island for our honeymoon, but first wanted to stop in and see Ellie and little Al at the hospital. She was in a large room with six beds separated by thin white curtains. The room smelled of disinfectant, and the grey-flecked tile floors shone up at us. The room was lined with windows on one side, and the mothers were in various states: some sleeping, some feeding their babies with the glass bottles the hospital provided, and some surrounded by family making a fuss over the new baby.

When we walked in, Ellie was beaming and holding the baby in her arms. She and the woman in the neighboring bed seemed to be comparing babies, which would inevitably lead to comparisons of which baby was more beautiful. Ellie's was. I was sure of it.

Ellie looked up and smiled. "Aren't you supposed to be on your way to the Beach Blanket Bingo honeymoon, there, Gidget?" Ellie's face was a little puffy, but she was glowing. I don't think I had ever seen her that happy, not even on her wedding day. She wore a white cotton robe with a little bow tied at the top. It was so beautiful, and I was sure she had made it. Leave it to Ellie to create a hospital wardrobe for the maternity ward.

"Yes, but not before I check on you and the baby."

"Look, Alice, your cousin Dot is here. Beware of this one. Her little adventures will get you into trouble." Alice had Al's nose but her mother's cheeks and eyes. She waved a tiny fist in the air, a gesture I'm sure was an opening to how she planned to rule the world, just like her mother and her grandmother did. Her eyes were new-baby blue and focused tightly on her mother.

"Is Al okay with not having a son?" I asked.

Ellie looked down into little Alice's eyes. "No need to worry about us. He's been crying like a baby over this little girl. Somehow, this change from boy to girl is amazing. It's like he wanted a daughter all along, and why not? She's the best thing we've ever done. Do you want to hold her? She won't bite, at least until she starts getting teeth."

"Can I?" I asked, a little unsure about holding a baby. I had done some babysitting when I was in my teens, but it had been a few years.

"You'd better get used to it. Right now, besides my mother, you're the only one I trust to babysit," Ellie said. She handed the little bundle of wiggles over to me.

At first a little shaky, I felt the warmth coming from the baby in my arms. Ben came up behind me and put a finger on her nose.

"Oh, you two are adorable," Ellie said. "I can't wait to see your first baby."

I started. "Now, wait a minute. We just got married. We're not ready for all that yet."

Ben grinned. "Not if you ask my mother. She's already planning the christening gown."

Little Alice reached up one hand and put it on my chin. My heart melted, but then I winked at Ben. "I'm nowhere near ready to have one of my own, but I have to admit, this child has some magical powers. I think I understand what all the fuss is about."

"Oh my. Alert the press," Ben said.

I handed the baby back to Ellie. "For now, it's a long-deserved vacation on the beach with nothing to worry about. Just me and Ben."

"That sounds pretty perfect to me," Ben nuzzled the back of my neck.

"Stop, you two," Ellie said. "Not in front of the baby. Just promise you'll stay out of trouble down there in South Texas."

"Of course we will," I said.

"I'll make sure of it," Ben answered. "We are going to be way too busy to investigate any murders."

"Famous last words," Ellie laughed.

A Note from the Author

Dear Readers,

Writing a book about wedding planning in 1965 was an adventure in itself. Looking through issues of *Bride's Magazine*, I knew I wanted Dot to have a Twiggy-inspired dress. Having a professional seamstress on hand was helpful, too. Cousin Ellie can sew anything, and in the book, she makes complete wardrobes while also handling a busy wedding season. She's also eight months pregnant, but Ellie doesn't slow down for much.

There really was a Cellar Bar in Fort Worth, and John F. Kennedy's security detail did visit it the night before the assassination. I'm not sure if it was as scandalous as Ellie described it, but the women did wear bikinis.

Dusty's claim to fame was real. The poor groundskeepers were forced to wear heavy space suits while performing tasks in the opening game of the Astrodome. I couldn't find the name of the person who thought of it, so for now, Dusty gets the credit.

After I wrote this book, I realized I had worked in just about every area of wedding planning. I've worked in flower shops, tuxedo shops (lots of hem sewing), newspapers (circulation) and churches. The most nerve-wracking was the tuxedo shop where we dealt with ring bearers who were measured in the fall and, because of a growth spurt, didn't fit in the suit in the spring, similar to what Ellie described for the flower girls.

Finally, when I worked in a church, there was a jack-of-all-trades caretaker who once told me, some people were the holy, holy, holies, and we were just the lowly, lowly, lowlies. It still makes me laugh.

—Teresa

Acknowledgments

I would like to thank Diane Krause, my friend and editor who kindly tells me she can't wait to read the next "Dot". Also, thank you to my critique group of many years. These ladies are never afraid to tell me when something isn't working and better yet when it is. Finally, thanks to Shawn and Deb at Level Best for all that you do!

About the Author

Teresa Trent has been writing and publishing mysteries since 2011, starting with the Pecan Bayou Mystery Series and followed by the Piney Woods Mystery Series. She presently writes the Swinging Sixties Mystery Series and the Henry Park Paranormal Series. When Teresa isn't writing novels and short stories, she spends her time creating narrated excerpts on her podcast, Books to the Ceiling, where she gets to use all that community theater experience from her teens and twenties, along with a little audio editing she learned from her daughter. Teresa is a former English teacher, but also spent many years teaching music to preschoolers, working with children of all abilities. Teresa makes her home in Texas with her husband and son.

AUTHOR WEBSITE:

  https://teresatrent.com

SOCIAL MEDIA HANDLES:

  FACEBOOK: https://www.facebook.com/teresatrentmysterywriter
  TWITTER: https://twitter.com/ttrent_cozymys
  BLOG: https://teresatrent.blog/ (Books to the Ceiling)
  WEBSITE: http://teresatrent.com
  GOODREADS: https://www.goodreads.com/author/show/5219581.Te

resa_Trent

INSTAGRAM: https://www.instagram.com/teresatrent_cozymys/
BOOKBUB: https://www.bookbub.com/profile/teresa-trent

Also by Teresa Trent

The Swinging Sixties Mystery Series Books 1-4

The Henry Park Mystery Series

The Piney Woods Mystery Series

The Pecan Bayou Mystery Series